"I was a virgin when I married."

Blaire laughed nervously. "Old-fashioned, huh? I feel like a damned neophyte. Especially around you."

"Why me especially?" Ruben asked.

Color seeped into her cheeks. "You seem like a man who's known a few women in the, uh, biblical sense."

He grinned and took her hand, stroking the center of her palm. "My share, but I think you're being too hard on yourself."

"Maybe," she conceded. His touch was doing crazy things to her. "But I am cautious with men. And that can be a turnoff."

"Not true."

"Not true, huh? Well, you haven't hit on me—except for that kiss the other night. And that wasn't premeditated. It was an accident."

"You make it sound like murder," Ruben murmured, pulling her into his arms. "Second-degree desire instead of first-degree lust." His lips settled on hers. "That kiss *wasn't* an accident. And neither is this...."

Imagine winning your very own butler for two weeks! That's the delightful premise behind **Delayne Camp**'s third Temptation novel. Butler Ruben Crosscroft is every woman's fantasy, a man who can cook and clean—and is sexy to boot! *Every* woman should have a Ruben, says Delayne, for two weeks if not for life!

Delayne has written more than thirty novels and is also published under the pen names Elaine Camp, Deborah Camp and Deborah Benet.

Books by Delayne Camp

Don't miss any of our special offers. Write to us at the following address for information on our newest releases.

Harlequin Reader Service
P.O. Box 1397, Buffalo, NY 14240
Canadian address: P.O. Box 603,
Fort Erie, Ont. L2A 5X3

The Butler Did It

DELAYNE CAMP

Harlequin Books

TORONTO • NEW YORK • LONDON
AMSTERDAM • PARIS • SYDNEY • HAMBURG
STOCKHOLM • ATHENS • TOKYO • MILAN
MADRID • WARSAW • BUDAPEST • AUCKLAND

Published July 1992

ISBN 0-373-25503-9

THE BUTLER DID IT

"I WON! I WON!"

Blaire Thomlin looked up from the illustration she'd been working on to see her daughter fly into her home studio.

"Good gracious!" Blaire held out her arms and Molly filled them, breathless and so excited her cheeks were rosy red. Molly's hair, black and cut pixie-fashion, lay in damp spikes on her forehead. Blaire plucked at her daughter's bangs and smiled, looking into her wide blue eyes. "What's all this about? Something great must have happened at school today."

"Not school," Molly said between gasping breaths. "This was in the mail." She waved a letter as if it were a victory flag. "I won him, Mom. Told you I'd win something someday."

"What have you won, sprout?" Blaire took the letter from Molly and glanced at the Miami return address, but she didn't recognize it. The letterhead, however, proudly proclaimed in Old English type: Silent Butler Silver Polish Company. "Let's see here," Blaire murmured, then read the letter aloud. "'Dear Ms. Thomlin—'"

"That's really me," Molly interrupted. "You had to fill out the form because I'm only eight and you had to be twenty-one to enter."

"Yes, I remember. You and your grandmother just can't pass up a chance to enter a contest, can you?"

"It's our hobby, Mom," Molly said. "It's fun, and I finally won something—somebody."

"*Somebody?*" Blaire ran her hand over Molly's hair, trying to tame the strands sticking up at her crown. "We, of Silent Butler Silver Polish Company, are pleased to inform you that you are the nationwide winner of our Butler For a Fortnight Contest," Blaire read, then paused to mull this over before continuing. "April 1 your butler will arrive at your St. Augustine, Florida, address, and you may make arrangements with him for his services for fourteen full days as promised in the contest rules." Blaire glanced quickly over the rest, amused at herself for thinking dirty. *His services, huh? Get your mind out of the gutter,* she scolded, but the wording tickled her fancy. "Is this a joke? There's got to be a catch. We couldn't have won a person."

"We did, Mom. It says so. I won him. My very own slave."

"Molly, you nut." Blaire tried to look stern even as visions of a bronzed god, genuflecting before her, flitted through her mind's eye. "He isn't a slave. He's a servant . . . a domestic."

"You pay for those, Mom. He's free—like a slave."

Blaire shook her head, unable to deal with a lecture on slavery and the problem this letter represented, at the same time. "I don't know about this, sprout. This guy is supposed to show up April 1—April Fool's Day. How appropriate." She looked at the calendar near her drafting table. "Oh, my gosh. That's—"

"Tomorrow," Molly supplied with a big grin. "Neat, huh?" Molly handed over the other mail. "We got this, too." Then she stood on tiptoe to survey her mother's sketch of a floppy-eared rabbit. "What are you working on?"

"The last few illustrations for *Donner Rabbit*," Blaire said, still studying the letter. *Has to be a catch*, she thought. Molly couldn't have won this contest. A butler. What the heck was she going to do if this turned out to be for real? She had a deadline, a birthday party and an ex-husband's visit scheduled next week. She couldn't add another aggravation to that stress-filled list.

"They've got to be done by next month?" Molly asked, still concerned with the children's book illustrations.

"What? Oh, those. Try next week. Two weeks, max." Blaire sighed and swiveled around on the stool to look at the art. During the past three years there had been a dramatic increase in her work. She'd been so busy she'd actually had to turn down a couple of assignments. Her housekeeping reflected this, she knew. There didn't seem to be much time for cleaning and cooking. A butler. She could certainly keep a maid busy for two weeks, but what did a butler do, exactly?

"Having a butler will be fun, huh, Mom? He'll help around here and you can work, work, work. And then there's my birthday next weekend." Molly rolled her baby blues toward Blaire in a suggestive way. "He can help with my party."

"It's just going to be family. Me, you, Grand and Pops, and your dad . . . if he makes it."

"He'll be here," Molly assured her with a blind faith found only in the young and the young-at-heart. "And with a butler here I could invite a bunch of friends."

"Molly..." Blaire said, making the word a warning.

"It wouldn't be any trouble for you, Mom. The butler will do it."

"Well, we'll see. Right now, I've got to finish up here and then call my agent in New York before she leaves the office." Blaire made a shooing motion. "Go change out of your school clothes. Put them in the clothes hamper," she instructed, noting smudges of dirt on the seat of Molly's slacks and what looked like drops of dried ketchup on her shirt. "We'll discuss this butler business later."

"There's nothing to discuss, is there?" Molly asked with a superior lift of her button nose. "I won him and he'll be here tomorrow."

Blaire frowned at Molly's back as she ran out of the studio, then read the letter again. Unbelievable, she thought. The little scamp had actually won a contest. A butler... Blaire sighed. Why did it have to be something that eats and talks? Why couldn't she have won a big-screen television or a jazzy sports car?

She couldn't say no to Molly—not this time. Her competitive daughter had been entering contests for a couple of years, encouraged by Blaire's own mother. Molly had never won anything before. Now that she had hit pay dirt, Blaire knew she couldn't deny Molly her winnings. She glanced at the calendar again. Tomorrow was Saturday, and she had a full day planned. Grocery shopping, laundry to be done, dry cleaning to pick up...she didn't have time for this! And hadn't her mother said something about dropping by? Well, she certainly couldn't hang around the house all day tomorrow, waiting for the guy to show up, Blaire thought. No way!

"A butler, for crying out loud!" Blaire groused, then began placing protective sheets over her drawings. *It's some kind of company come-on, so don't waste another minute worrying about it,* she told herself.

"Mom?"

Blaire glanced over her shoulder at Molly.

"You won't send him away if he shows up, will you? I mean, I *can* keep him, can't I?" Molly essayed her most convincing woe-is-mistreated-me expression.

Blaire's heart softened. "Yes," she said, laughing when Molly jumped up and down in a burst of joy. "But don't get your hopes up, because chances are he'll be a no-show. This whole thing is most likely a sales pitch by the company. And I warn you—" she paused to raise a cautionary finger "—if the company says I have to buy something before we can get this butler, then the deal is off. You understand, Molly Amelia?"

"Yes, Mom," Molly said in a singsong tone. "But he'll be here—no strings attached."

"Let me fill you in on something we gals discover, one way or another." Blaire cupped her daughter's chin to angle Molly's gaze up to hers. "*All* men come with strings attached."

AWAKENED BY A DISTANT chiming, Blaire sat up in bed and flung back the top sheet. She glanced at the clock and moaned when she saw it was only eight.

"It's Saturday," she grumbled, wondering who in the world dared awaken her on a weekend morning. The doorbell rang again. Blaire pushed her feet into fuzzy slippers and grabbed her short robe from off the back of the vanity chair. She belted it around her waist as she shuffled from the bedroom to the living room. The hem of her hunter green robe stopped five inches above her knees, barely concealing her nightshirt.

Blaire rose up on tiptoes to press one eye against the peephole. The vestiges of sleep sailed away with the vision of a handsome face. She didn't know him, but she wished she did. Tall, dark-haired and blue-eyed, he stood erect and fingered the knot of his striped tie. When he lifted a hand to ring the bell again, Blaire snapped out of her peeping Thomasina routine.

"Who is it?" Blaire asked through the door.

"It's Ruben Crosscroft from Silent Butler Silver Polish Company, madam. I believe you are the lucky winner? Ms. Thomlin, isn't it?"

"Oh, my gosh!" Blaire closed her eyes and leaned her forehead against the door, acclimatizing herself to the bold, masculine fact standing on her porch. The butler had arrived! Dazed, she unlocked the front door and opened it. He looked even better than before. Morning sunlight picked up the silver highlights in his temples. She'd expected a proper old gent with a stiff upper lip. But this guy! This guy was a first-class hunk in a three-piece suit.

His blue-eyed gaze lingered on Blaire's tanned legs. "I seem to have awakened you. I'm terribly sorry." His accent was the only thing she'd expected—British. Veddy British.

"You're from England?"

"I've lived there, yes, but I'm an Australian by birth."

Australian? Like Mel Gibson? Like Bryan Brown? She shook her head, knowing her thoughts were headed for dangerous territory. "Yes, you did get me out of bed," she told him. "So can you please come back at a decent hour? Say, sometime around noon?" She was at a decided disadvantage in her robe and slippers while tall, dark and handsome stood there like a cover model from *GQ*.

"I see." He glanced over his shoulder at the empty street. "I'm afraid I've let the cab go, but I can sit out here—" he examined the three narrow concrete steps leading to the porch "—and wait until you're ready to receive company."

Blaire glared at him, miffed that he'd backed her into a corner. She surrendered and swept an arm with a flourish. "Enter. We'll talk. Just don't expect me to be gracious. I'm grumpy before I get two cups of coffee inside me." When he started toward the threshold, Blaire flattened one hand against his chest. "Before this goes any further, may I see some identification?" She held out her hand.

"But of course." He reached inside his suit jacket and produced a letter from the company, his driver's license and a copy of a diploma from a trade school in England. Blaire noted that the degree was in Culinary Expertise and Domestic Management, of all things. "I have credit cards and—"

"This is enough," Blaire said, handing the items back to him. "You're legitimate."

"My mother thanks you for that assessment."

His jab of humor sent a rueful smile to her lips. His cobalt-blue eyes laughed at her. She noticed the cleft in the underside of his chin, and found it distracting—attractively so.

"Crosscroft," she said, trying out his name. "Ruben Crosscroft. Quite a handle you've got there. Unreal, made up, right?"

"I assure you it isn't made up," Ruben said. "Like me, it's legitimate."

"And you're Australian."

"By birth. I'm an American citizen. I have been since I was twenty-one. I'm thirty-three now, madam."

"Please, don't call me that," Blaire said, wrinkling her nose. Belatedly, she wondered why he'd provided his age. Did he expect the same from her? "I'm Blaire Thomlin. My daughter, Molly Jacobs, is the one who actually entered the contest. It's a hobby of hers. You're the first prize she ever won."

"Molly Jacobs?" he asked.

"I'm divorced from her father," Blaire explained.

"And you kept your maiden name?"

"That's right." She looked at him squarely, wondering if she'd earned his disapproval. Meaning to head him off at the pass, she added, "I saw no reason in exchanging my family name for his. I know it's traditional, but I'm not much on rules and unquestioned—"

"Bully for you," he said smoothly. His generous mouth tipped up on one side in a lopsided grin. "I'm proud of my family name as well and wouldn't want to discard it." He flicked back his cuff, checking the time. "And as for rules, well, they generally cramp one's style." He held out one hand. "So good to make your acquaintance, Ms. Thomlin."

She inched her hand into his. His handshake was firm and polite. Blaire looked deeply into his eyes. She liked what she saw, and in that instant, she knew the feeling was mutual. Something sexual sizzled between them. Blaire broke contact first, pulling her hand from his, feeling her color rise. She'd been divorced for four years, and this was the first man to fluster her, make her heart race, heat the blood in her veins. And he was a butler, a grand prize. Suddenly, she was glad they'd won him instead of a fancy sports car.

Blaire glanced down at her robe. She looked like a rumpled sheet, she thought, combing her hair with her fingers. "I didn't think you'd actually show. It was the April Fool's Day part that made me think the whole thing was a joke."

"That angle hadn't occurred to me. You don't still think I'm part of some elaborate joke, do you?"

"No . . . I—I guess not." She shrugged off the last of her suspicions and glanced around at the muted sunshine spilling through the weave in the floor-length draperies pulled across the patio door. "Well, have a seat."

"May I prepare coffee and breakfast for you and Molly?"

"Coffee's already made. I have a timer on it," she explained. "Would you like a cup?" She waved him off when he made a move toward the kitchen. "Sit. I'll get it."

Blaire escaped into the kitchen and used the shiny, reflective surface of the toaster as a mirror. She combed her blond hair with her fingers again, then washed her hands and prepared a coffee tray. When she rejoined him, he had pulled back the draperies at the patio door and stood there gazing at the spring day.

"This is a beautiful area," he said, only then turning to look at her. "Have you lived here long?"

"Yes, most of my life." She set the tray on the low sofa table. "How long have you been a butler?"

"Not too awfully long. Actually, I was a butler for only a short time a couple of years ago. Lately, I've been concentrating on my culinary talents. I want to be a chef."

"Oh, is that so?" She motioned for him to be seated again. "So, butlering isn't your thing. Why did you take on this job?" She found herself looking for a chink in his armor. There must be something disgusting about him—some despicable thing. After all, he's a man, she thought. He's got to have strings.

"For the money. I'm trying to gather funds to open my own restaurant. Possibly right here in St. Augustine." He tasted the brew, grimaced and added a heaping spoonful of sugar. Another taste. He added milk.

Blaire regarded him frostily, fighting off feelings of inadequacy. So her coffee wasn't a prizewinner. It was hot and the right color, meeting her requirements. "What, exactly, does a butler do?" she asked when he'd set the coffee mug away from him.

"Traditionally, a butler captains the domestic crew."

"This crew consists of me and Molly." She shrugged.

"But my job description includes cooking, cleaning and managing the household. In short—" he smiled, showing off shallow dimples "—your wish is my command."

Blaire choked on her sip of coffee, but recovered quickly. That's when she noticed that her heart had increased its pace and blood was singing in her ears. *Get a grip,* she warned herself, but she found it difficult to keep her cool. Mischief lurked in his eyes and at the corners of his wide mouth. She felt a stutter coming on, so she held her tongue until she could trust it again.

"When I received that letter yesterday saying you were coming, I thought you'd be a big inconvenience, but then I started thinking . . ."

"And you've changed your mind?"

"Yes, sort of. As it happens, I have a busy schedule the next two weeks. There's Molly's birthday, and I've got a deadline—"

"Deadline for what? Are you a writer?"

"No, an illustrator for children's books."

"How interesting." He seemed genuinely impressed. His gaze drifted to her hands. "You have an artist's hands. I should have noticed before."

Blaire glanced at her hands, having never thought of them as distinctive. His compliment acted on her like a good stiff drink, and she had to stifle a giggle. "Can you manage a birthday party?" she asked, purposefully steering the conversation back to business.

"Of course. I think you'll find me quite capable, Ms. Thomlin. I've had precious few complaints."

I'll bet, Blaire thought, admiring his hands, which were long-fingered, blunt-ended, with clean, short nails. He had a great tan. A Florida tan. "Where do you live?"

"I was living in Palm Beach. Your daughter will be how old?"

"Nine next Saturday. It'll be a small party. Just a few friends and family." Palm Beach, Blaire noted. High-dollar neighborhoods. "I never dreamed Molly would actually win this contest. Granted, I could use an extra pair of hands around here, but . . ." She looked at her stereo, her television and video player. This man could steal her blind the moment her back was turned. She had learned the hard way not to trust, not to believe every sincerely spoken word. Her ex-husband had been a masterful liar. "You know, I was thinking, what if you accidentally break something, or what if—"

"I'm fully bonded and insured by the Silent Butler company." He handed her an insurance certificate. "That's your copy to keep."

Blaire took the paper, feeling better about having him around. She could use a personable child-sitter and household organizer for two whole weeks, and he certainly wasn't hard to look at. In fact, it was all she could do not to stare at him with lust in her heart. Her critical eye caught sight of dust on the television and bits of lint on the carpet. House cleaning had never been her favorite thing. Besides, it seemed that the older Molly got, the more time Blaire had to devote to mothering and chauffeuring. There weren't enough hours in the day anymore.

"I'm quite good with children. I'd be all too happy to arrange Molly's party," he offered. "I certainly understand how a single mother can be so busy she meets herself coming and going."

"Sold." Blaire slapped her thighs decisively, then yanked the sides of her robe closer together when she noticed him looking at her bustline. "That is, you've convinced me that you're manna from heaven, Mr. Crosscroft. When can you begin work? Why don't I just call you Ruben and you can call me Blaire?"

"I can start right away, Blaire." He glanced toward the door leading to the bedroom wing. "Might you have a spare bedroom?"

Oops. There's that string. She knew he was too good to be true. "Yes, so what?"

"I was thinking I might be a live-in butler."

"Live-in?" Actually being roommates with him might be too much of a good thing. "Can't you stay in a hotel or something? Surely the company is paying your expenses."

"Well, yes." He sat forward and studied his clasped hands. The scent of lemon-lime wafted from him to Blaire. He'd had a close shave, but Blaire could still make out the outline of his beard. "I was hoping to save the expense money. You see, I'm pinching every penny because I'm on the verge of opening my own restaurant. I took this position with Silent Butler because the money I will make—the salary *and* the expense account—is sufficient to lease space and get my business started."

"I admire your ambition, but—"

"By living here, I'll be at your beck and call round the clock. The rules dictate that I be on duty only eight hours a day." He inched closer, giving her a wink. "But you and I love to shatter rules, don't we?"

Blaire laughed under her breath, feeling nervous and uncertain. The man was too hunky and too devious for her own good.

"There's a property for lease in St. Augustine I'm looking into. It would be perfect, but I'll need every cent to secure it."

"Look, I work in my home, and I can't be—"

"By living here I won't disturb you at indecent hours like these. You can sleep in any time you want," he interrupted, then flashed a grin meant to charm. It did.

Blaire felt hot all over. Too young for a hot flash, she thought, so this must be that old black magic. Heaven help her! His argument was sound, but she hesitated. Having a man living with her, even for two weeks, sent trepidation through her. The last time a man had shared her home, she'd been married and it hadn't been pretty. Oh, there had been moments, but mostly she recalled the disarray of her life back then. Living with will-o'-the-wisp Jimmy Jacobs had been like a roller coaster ride—there were thrilling moments, but mostly you felt sick inside.

"What say?" Ruben asked, his phrasing earning a smile from her. "Have we a deal?"

The doorbell chimed, and Ruben reacted before Blaire could move a muscle, reminding her of a punch-drunk prizefighter bursting to life at the sound of any bell. He opened the door and dipped his head, acknowledging the caller. Standing behind him, Blaire stifled a groan. Her mother! She loved her mother to death, but at times—like now—she thought her mother would be the death of *her.*

"Good morning," he said cheerfully. "May I help you, madam?"

"That's the best offer I've had this morning," Agatha Thomlin said, focusing her catlike eyes on Ruben. "If you mean what you say, I have a list—"

"Mother!" Blaire stepped forward to stop Agatha from any further outrageous flirtation, which happened to be her mother's favorite pastime. "Come in. What in the world are you doing here at this hour? It's Saturday. Didn't anybody but me notice that?"

"Chill out, Blaire," her mother said, gliding past Ruben into the living room. "Your father rose before dawn to go fishing near here, and since I was already up, I decided to get an early start. I told you I was going to drop by today, so don't look so put out. There's an art show near the first settlement area that Molly must see." Agatha's green eyes slid to Ruben again. "St. Augustine is the oldest town in the U.S., stranger. We haven't met, have we?"

"No, but you're Blaire's mother, I take it."

"Among other things, yes." Agatha beamed at him. "Are you married? I am, of course, but I was asking for my daughter's—"

"Down, Mother," Blaire said with carefully crafted sarcasm. "Ruben Crosscroft, this is my mother Agatha Thomlin. Ruben is—"

"Australian?" Agatha asked.

"Good ear," Ruben praised her. "Most people think I'm English."

"Do most people think you're gorgeous, too?"

"Mother, please." Blaire laughed, shaking her finger at her. "I'll go get Molly."

"Grand!" Molly came running. "Is Pops with you?" Molly stopped when she saw Ruben. She folded her arms across the front of her nightshirt. "Oh, hi."

"Molly, this is Ruben Crosscroft," Blaire said, watching her daughter's face carefully as she delivered the next news, "Your butler."

"Butler?" Molly's eyes widened, and a delightful smile overtook her features. "For real?"

"For real," Blaire assured her.

"Wow! Grand, I won him in a contest."

"Did you now?" Agatha arched one flame-colored brow. "I've been entering contests for years and I never won anything like *this!*"

Molly came closer, suddenly shy. "Can we keep him, Mom?"

"Yes, sprout. Ruben, this is Molly."

Ruben held out his hand and shook Molly's. "So pleased to make your acquaintance, Miss Molly."

Molly giggled, her face turning pink. Blaire knew the feeling. "Isn't he neat, Grand?"

"He certainly is," Agatha agreed. "She calls me Grand because I am," she explained to Ruben. "Pops, of course, is my husband Dexter. I call him—"

"Mother, please," Blaire begged to no avail.

"—Sexy Dexy," Agatha finished with a satisfied smile. "Because he is. I believe you and my husband would have much in common, Ruben."

"Molly," Blaire said, frantic to find order in the chaos, "why don't you show Ruben around the house and grounds while I talk to Grand."

"Okay." Molly took his hand in hers. "I'll show you my swing set first. It's out back. I've got a fort out there, too. Grand, don't leave without me."

"I won't, dear."

When the patio door slid shut behind Molly and the butler, Blaire turned around to face her mother's blatant curiosity.

"Well?" Agatha goaded, tapping one foot and toying with the rope of pearls around her neck. Her olive eyes swept Blaire from head to toe, missing nothing, filling in the blanks. "Is he an awesome Aussie or is he an awesome Aussie? Dear, your luck is changing. I do believe you've hit the jackpot with this one."

2

WITH MOLLY PULLING on his left index finger, Ruben allowed himself to be guided to the backyard swing set.

"Would you like for me to push you?" he asked.

"Sure." Molly hopped onto one swing, grabbed the chains on either side, and let out a giggle as Ruben sent her soaring. "I'm flying!"

Ruben indulged in a few minutes of childish pleasure. He couldn't recall his last trip on a swing, but he'd probably been in his early teens. He surveyed the yard; it was a family place. A fort had been erected in one corner. A redwood picnic table and benches were positioned near an outdoor barbecue. He noticed a gate set in the middle of the back fence.

"Molly, is that the way to the beach?" He pointed to the gate.

"Yeah. Want to walk to it? It's right over that rise."

"Would your mother mind?"

"No, not as long as you go with me. I just can't go alone."

"Good, then let's. I love the beach and the ocean, and St. Augustine has such a lovely shoreline."

Walking side by side, Ruben examined Molly's cute profile. She had a few of her mother's features, but Ruben guessed she looked more like her father.

"Does your dad live around here?"

"No, he lives in Texas now...I think. He moves around a lot. He's a football player."

"Really? For which team?"

"He's in between teams right now."

"Do you see him often?"

"Not really. But he visits when he can. He calls every month."

"Does your mom date much? Does she have a boyfriend?" He felt like a complete cad for pumping the kid for information, but he also guessed that Blaire would give out scant personal data, and he wanted to know her current status. Not only was she going to be his boss for the next two weeks, she was a beautiful boss.

"She dates, but she doesn't have a steady boyfriend. Just friends, she says. Nobody she wants to marry." Molly spotted a shaggy, sandy-colored dog and raced ahead. "It's Omar! He belongs to a neighbor. Omar, come here, boy!"

While Molly frolicked with the dog, Ruben appreciated the view they'd come upon. White, sugary sand stretched to a foaming ocean, white-capped on this windy morning. Only half a dozen people strolled the shoreline, some hunting for shells. Molly threw a tennis ball and laughed as the dog swam out to retrieve it.

He could settle in quite comfortably here, Ruben thought. It was so unlike Palm Beach, and he liked that. Life was simpler here, and people weren't as concerned with who was messing with who and how much money so-and-so was awarded in the last settlement. It was hard to recall, but there had been a time when he'd enjoyed the jet-set life-style. He'd wanted it. He'd gone after it. And, by gum, he'd gotten it. In spades. A shudder broke in him, and the word, that word he had come to hate—*gigolo*—burned up and down his mind. Ruben rubbed his face, making his skin tingle. He felt a need to run, so he jogged closer to the lapping waves where Molly played with Omar.

"You enter lots of contests?" he asked, watching the hound swim into the whitecaps.

"Every one I see," Molly said. "Grand got me started. She's been entering them for years. She won a trip to Hawaii once, and she's won appliances . . . a microwave, cameras, blenders, stuff like that." She turned her happy smile on him. "But you're the bestest prize ever, Ruben. I can call you that, right?"

He nodded and rested a hand on top of her shiny hair. "Do you think your mom will let me bunk in the guest room?"

"Probably. Grand will talk her into it." Molly glanced over her shoulder in the direction of the house. "Grand's probably doing that right now."

"I'll keep my fingers crossed."

"You like being a butler?"

He shrugged. "Not really, but I think being your butler will be fun. What I really want to do is own a restaurant. I might just open one in St. Augustine."

"That'd be neat. So you cook good, huh?"

"Very good. What kind of food do you like?"

"Cheeseburgers and fries. Can you cook those?"

Ruben laughed and ruffled Molly's black hair. "You bet, mate. What does your mom like to eat?"

"I dunno. Everything, I guess."

Ruben started to ask another question about Blaire, but stopped himself. *Habits die hard*, he thought, realizing he had launched into his we-aim-to-please routine. Find out the lady's likes and dislikes and then mold yourself into her perfect companion. He'd done it so often it had become second nature. But no more, he vowed. From here on in he would please himself. After this little stint as butler, he'd be calling the shots in his life, and he could hardly wait.

"Maybe we should head back." He ran his gaze over Molly's nightshirt. "You might catch a sniffle."

"Are you married?" Molly asked, slipping her hand into his.

"No, are you?"

She giggled. "No, silly. Do you have a girlfriend?"

"Not anymore."

"But you did?"

He nodded. Thinking of Earla as a girlfriend seemed odd. She wasn't the girlfriend type. His thoughts circled back to his new employer. Now there was a woman who was the girlfriend type. A man could take Blaire Thomlin home to Mother and just know that Mum would be crazy about her, Dad would welcome her into the family, and everyone would agree she was a great catch. Normally, he wouldn't put so much stock in first impressions, but he felt he could trust his intuition this time. Blaire Thomlin was a decent person, a loving mother, and a woman who deserved a good man.

Did that leave him out? Ruben wondered, then steeled himself against such negative thinking. Just because he'd fallen into a bad situation in Palm Beach, didn't mean he was a rounder in every sense of the word. He chastised himself for sizing up Blaire as a sexual partner right off the bat. Force of habit, he thought, but something deep down told him it was more than that. Something deep down whispered that he'd be hard-pressed to think of Blaire Thomlin in any other way. After all, she had a mouth made for kissing and curves made for caressing.

He glanced at Molly skipping beside him. Blaire also had an eight-year-old daughter, he reminded himself. He looked ahead as the house came into view. And Blaire had a mortgage, a career, roots, a real, American life. She had all the things he'd never had, but had dreamed of lately. She'd probably tell him he'd have to find a hotel room, that she didn't want a stranger moving in for two weeks, contest or no contest.

"I want to show you my fort, then my bedroom," Molly said, grabbing his hand again. "Then I'll show you your room."

Ruben smiled. *From Molly's lips to God's ears*, he thought.

DRESSED IN JEANS and a shirt, Blaire sat at the kitchen table with her mother and nursed her second cup of coffee. Out the window, Blaire caught sight of Molly and Ruben walking over the rise toward the beach. Agatha sipped from a glass of tomato juice. As usual, she was dressed in jewel tones, flamboyant and artsy. Blaire didn't think her mother would ever grow or look old. She was young at heart, and it shone through and through.

Agatha twisted around to see what had snared Blaire's attention. When she faced Blaire again, she laughed lightly. "A butler, huh? Molly must be thrilled to have finally won a contest."

"I never thought she would, but I admit I *did* have a few flights of fancy about winning a cool million or maybe a sports car or a vacation home. A butler, I never imagined."

"Thank God he's to die for," Agatha said. "Wouldn't it have been tragic if he was some dusty relic with his nose out of joint?"

"There's a glitch . . ." Blaire paused, finding a better phrase. "A string attached, naturally. He wants to live here. He wants the spare bedroom."

Agatha nodded expectantly. "Uh-huh, so what's the glitch?"

"I just told you, Mother. He wants to live here with me and Molly."

"That's the string? Having a hunk around the place—one eager to take orders from you—sounds like a perk to me."

"Will you for once behave like a mother instead of a wanton artist?"

"I *am* a wanton artist," Agatha insisted, her gaze moving pointedly to her signed oil hanging in Blaire's kitchen, depicting a heavy-breasted dark-skinned woman bathing in a sun-prismed creek. "And a damned good one, I might add. But as your mother, I think you live like an Amazon warrior with a kid in tow."

Blaire laughed bitterly. "Thanks ever so much for that flattering assessment, Mother."

"Just because you married a rotter, doesn't mean you have to strap on the chastity belt. This Ruben fellow looks to be fun and virile. It's a combination I can highly recommend, being married to Sexy Dexy."

"Ruben Crosscroft is a butler, Mother, not the resident stud."

"No reason why he couldn't be both. I bet he could handle the load." She winked, then laughed at Blaire's annoyance. "Lighten up, dear. Look upon this as an adventure."

"I don't need one of those, thank you. Mother, what if this guy is a kidnapper, a pervert, a con artist? Huh, what about that? I mean, he could be *anybody*. He could harbor any assortment of psychopathic tendencies."

Agatha shrugged, but Blaire could see she'd aroused suspicion. "He looks honest to me. About thirty, isn't he?"

"Thirty-three, or so he says."

"Blaire," Agatha chided, "don't be so quick to assume everyone is lying. Ever since your marriage, you've grown progressively pessimistic." She sipped her juice. "Let him have the extra room." Agatha held up a hand to stop Blaire's next attack. "And I'll call your father and have him do a check."

"Can he do that? I mean, Dad's not on the force anymore."

"A retired police captain has many favors he can call in, dear. Dex is no exception. He'll have your butler thoroughly checked out for your peace of mind."

"I'd rather know he's okay before I tell him he can move in."

"All right, all right." Her mother rose from the chair and went to the blue kitchen phone. She punched in a number, then put her hand over the receiver. "Your father is fishing, as I told you, but I can beep him." Blaire

nodded and poured herself another cup of coffee while
her mother arranged for the electronic signal. She located a Twinkie and tore into the package, offered her
mother one, and was glad when Agatha turned up her
nose at the spongy pastry. Blaire had finished off one
of them when the phone rang. Her mother answered it.

"Hello, Dex. No, nothing's wrong. I just want you
to run a check on someone. Someone in your daughter's life." Agatha laughed lightly. "Well, this is a man.
Yes, you heard me right."

Blaire rolled her eyes, annoyed, and bit into the next
Twinkie while her mother spelled Ruben's name to her
father and tossed out a few other bits of information
about the butler. When Agatha replaced the receiver,
she sent Blaire a smug smile.

"Your father will get right on it. He'll know something within the hour, most likely. It's a simple thing to
find out if Ruben has a record or not, and that's the
main thing you'll want to know."

"That, and if he's a fugitive from some institution
back in Great Britain."

"I'm sure Dex will check with Interpol, too." She
drank the last of her juice. "Is Molly's father coming
here for her birthday?"

Blaire nodded. "Jimmy sent a postcard from Texas.
He said he'd be here, but you know how that goes. You
can't depend on him for anything."

"What's he doing in Texas? He's not working, is he?"

"Jimmy?" Blaire laughed, mirthlessly. "Surely you
jest, Mother. Last time he called Molly he said something about interviewing for an assistant coaching job
with the Dallas Cowboys."

It was Agatha's turn to laugh hollowly. "In his dreams. In his dreams!"

Blaire lifted one shoulder. "It must be hard to be a has-been. I feel sorry for him."

"Has-been? He played professional football for two seasons—that is, he was *signed* to play. He sat on the bench, mostly. I don't think he ever qualified as a has-got, so he can't very well be a has-been. What happened to that woman he was living with in Chicago?"

"Guess she broke up with him. He didn't mention her. He probably has someone new in his life by now. Jimmy hates being alone." Blaire stared out the window, her memories of Jimmy making her uneasy. So much of her life with Jimmy had been full of anxiety that it was hard for her to think of him without getting angry or feeling hurt. Would she ever get over her failed marriage? Would she ever be able to think of it dispassionately?

"You need a man in your life, Blaire," Agatha said, as if reading her mind. "Every time Jimmy's mentioned, you frown. You're still smarting from the wounds inflicted, and it's high time those wounds were healed. Over and done with." Agatha snapped her fingers, illustrating her point. "Only another man can do that. You've got to have new memories—good memories to blot out the old ones."

The phone rang and Agatha answered it. It was Dex. When she hung up, she looked triumphant.

"Clean as a hound's tooth. Guess you have a roomie for the week."

Blaire sighed, unsure how to take the news. "That was fast work. Dad's positive?"

"It's the computer age, dear. Your father is thorough in everything. If he says Ruben is clean, you can throw out the soap." Agatha smiled cunningly. "Your Ruben Crosscroft is full of confidence, and I admire that."

"He's not mine . . . and how do you know he's confident?"

"I noticed his two suitcases outside before I came in. He stashed them discreetly behind the chinaberry bush, but I spotted them."

Blaire glared out the window, spotting Ruben and Molly coming back from their beach stroll. "That doesn't endear him to me. I've a good mind to tell him to rent himself a hotel room."

"But you won't because your mama didn't raise no fools." Agatha stood and pulled her car keys from her leather clutch purse. "You get Molly dressed and I'll take her with me so you can get your butler all settled in."

"Mother, stop it."

"Stop what?"

Blaire glared at her. "Stop calling him mine and stop smiling at me as if you arranged all of this and everything's going your way." She brought herself up short. "You *didn't* arrange this, did you? I mean, this isn't your idea of an April Fool's joke?"

Agatha shook her head, retaining her mysterious smile. "No. Not even I could think up such a scrumptious surprise for you." She moved slowly from the kitchen to the patio door. "Enjoy him, Blaire. You have a butler—free of charge. Let him clean and cook and—whatever he does best." She opened the sliding glass door and a sea breeze billowed her silk blouse and artfully draped skirt. The cry of gulls came winging into the room. "This is a fantasy for most women, not an inconvenience." Her sigh was a performance. "If I didn't have your father, I'd like to be inconvenienced by Ruben Crosscroft."

Blaire closed her eyes, feeling a headache coming on.

AFTER SEEING MOLLY and Agatha off, Blaire returned to the living room to find Ruben sorting through her cassette collection. She cleared her throat and he executed a crisp about-face.

"You like classical. Me, too."

Blaire's smile felt stiff on her lips. Why was she so nervous? The answer came to her in a flash. "Look, I've never had ser—domestics around before. I don't really know what's expected of me. Do you think the contest people will come around and want pictures and interviews?"

"Toward the end of my tenure, yes. But they won't require more than an hour or two of your time. Less, if you want." His gaze turned to his suitcases. "Could you show me to my room so I can stow my things?"

"Oh, sure." She bobbed a shoulder and moved jerkily to the guest room, excruciatingly aware of his soft tread right behind her.

For his part, Ruben eyed her bottom with great respect. There was nothing more pleasing to his eye than the heart-shape of a woman's backside, and Blaire's was perfection encased in sky-blue denim. A little piece of heaven, he mused, barely smothering a chuckle. She flung open a door at the far end of the hall and went inside first.

"This is it, such as it is. As you can see, I use it as a sewing room, catch-all room, junk room. But there's a bed and table and lamp. Closet is over here." She crossed to it and slid back the double louvered doors to reveal a collection of odds and ends. "I can shift some of this stuff—restack the piles, you know, and come up with enough space for your clothes and shoes."

"Allow me. That's what I'm here for."

She laughed under her breath and went to open the top drawer of a dresser. "It's going to take some getting used to, not to think of you as a guest. Just cram the stuff in this top drawer into the others and you can have this space all to yourself." She waved a careless hand that managed to brush across his chest. Blaire jerked back as if he'd burned her. "I . . . sorry. Anyway, these things are overflow, so don't worry about them. I should go through all this and give most of it to the Goodwill."

"I can help with that, too."

"Not this coming week," she said. "I've got too much on my plate as it is."

"Then you're lucky to have me." He wanted to wink at her, but refrained. She was as nervous as a deer on a fall morning. "This will do nicely." He set his suitcases beside the double bed.

"I hope you don't smoke. Molly's allergic to—"

"I don't. Never have. Don't wish to."

"This room is small," she said, glancing around apprehensively. "Maybe you'd rather go to a hotel and—"

"It's fine. Certainly big enough for me."

"Well, the bathroom is right there." She pointed toward it, located between the guest room and Molly's room. "I have a private bath off my bedroom. Oh, by the way, I shower in the morning and so does Molly."

"Then I'll shower in the evenings. I won't get in your way." He couldn't help but indulge in a moment's fantasy of her, tanned and glowing and dripping wet.

"I don't keep any liquor in the house, and I don't ap—"

"I've never acquired much of a taste for liquor," he said, heading her off. "Other than the occasional bottle of fine wine to complement an exceptional dinner, I'm a teetotaler."

"Perfect," she said between clenched teeth, thinking that the man was impossibly companionable. "You're going to make me feel like an inferior being, if you don't watch out."

"Inferior? I didn't mean to . . ."

"I know, I know." She laughed and headed down the hall. "Don't worry. I don't *really* believe for a minute that you're perfect, but I congratulate you on your convincing performance." The glance she tossed him over her shoulder glimmered with mischief. "This is Molly's room. I expect her to keep it tidy, but she needs help, as you can see."

He poked his head inside. Toys littered the center of the floor, dolls mostly. A few clothes had been thrown haphazardly onto a chair. The bed hadn't been made yet. "Not too terrible," he said, judging it would take him less than an hour to set the room straight.

"Don't you hate cleaning up after other people? I can hardly stand picking up after me and my daughter. I can't imagine doing it for strangers."

Ruben looked at her, surprised to see that she expected an answer and actually was interested in what he had to say. He'd been raised by parents who made their livings as domestics, and he'd done his fair share of such work, but this was the first employer who had ever sought his opinion, his feelings on servitude.

"It's not so bad," he said, choosing his words carefully. "It's not what I want to do the rest of my life, but it's not too terribly awful. Especially for people like you and Molly. You seem to be quite neat."

"Neat? Lordy, you must have worked for some real slobs if you think my house is neat."

He laughed with her. "I've seen worse, believe me. In fact, I daresay, my own place has looked atrocious."

"And where is that?" she asked. "Your place...where do you live?"

He thought of the guest house he'd occupied on Earla's impressive estate. "Nowhere right now. I'm relocating."

"Oh, yes. You're thinking of opening a restaurant. You went to trade school or something."

"Yes, in London. I learned all kinds of domestic work there, but I concentrated on the chef and management classes."

"I'll come to your restaurant when it opens," Blaire promised.

"I'll count on that."

The overhead light shimmered over his thick, slightly wavy hair. It was as black as Molly's, but with touches of silver at the temples. No doubt he'd age to perfection, Blaire thought with a twinge of envy. Being blond, she found dark hair attractive. She liked the way silver shone in his. Blondes just dulled and had to rely on expensive hair colorings. Brunettes shimmered naturally as they grew older.

"So, you're not married." Blaire blinked, surprised by her own question. Where had *that* come from?

"No, not married. No kids, no wives—ex or otherwise. I'd like to settle down, though. I've been fairly footloose." He bit off the rest, reminding himself that this woman wouldn't find his past admirable. *She'll kick you out if you tell her you used to moonlight as an escort for monied women,* an inner voice assured him, and he heeded it. "I...uh, that is, I've been gaining chef experience. I goofed off a lot in my twenties, and now I'm having to make up for lost time. The restaurant business is a real rat race, and I'm lagging behind."

Blaire opened the last door, giving Ruben a glimpse of satin and lace inside a bedroom that smelled of expensive perfume. "You haven't butlered in a while?"

"No, not in quite a while, but I assure you, I'm fully qualified." He craned forward, wanting a better look at her private quarters. "Is this—?"

"My bedroom," she finished for him. "So, it's been some time since you were a kept man?" Blaire grinned, tickled by her choice of phrases and the implications.

"What's *that* mean?" Ruben's voice was so harsh, so different from its usual lightness, that Blaire jerked a little and her gaze swung about to him. He looked shaken, on the verge of anger.

"S-sorry," she said, her mouth suddenly dry. "I was just joking, trying to be funny." She closed the door, cutting off his view of her bed. "Look, I've got some errands to run. Why don't you settle into your room while I'm gone?"

"Mightn't I go with you? Perhaps I could even do the errands for you. I have a chauffeur's license."

"No, I . . . I'll do them. I want to get out for a while." She hurried along the hallway. "I'll probably be back before Mother brings Molly home."

"Very well."

"Just make yourself at home." She grabbed her purse and car keys. "We'll both go to the grocery store tomorrow when we get back from church. Okay?"

"Whenever you wish."

She stopped at the front door to look back at him. A smile played at the corner of her mouth. "My wish is your command?" She laughed before he could answer. "Somehow, you're not what I pictured when I read the story of the genie in the bottle." She wiggled the fingers of one hand. "See you later."

Ruben stood at the front door and watched her leave in a shiny blue Mustang convertible. *Kept man.* He went back inside and slammed the door behind him.

3

AFTER CHURCH AND LUNCH the next day, Blaire and Molly climbed into Dex and Agatha's station wagon for the ride home. Agatha removed a vial from her purse and sprayed the interior of the vehicle with Passion perfume.

"Dex, if you ever put another container of that awful-smelling stink bait in this car, I'll brain you," she complained, sniffing and then wrinkling her nose. "I can still smell it."

"Aw, honey. How can I catch catfish without stink bait?"

"Find a way." Agatha turned sideways to look back at Molly and Blaire. "So, how did you like having a butler yesterday?"

"I told you, Mother. It was fine." Blaire stared out the window at the blurred scenery. Actually, the evening had been uncomfortable for her. After getting Molly off to bed, Blaire had done something she rarely did—she'd gone to her room, closed the door and read until midnight. Having a man under her roof again had proved unsettling. "Oh, I forgot to tell you that the contest sponsor called last night to make sure Ruben had arrived."

"Yeah, and they're going to take pictures and stuff later," Molly added.

"Pictures?" Dex asked, looking at Blaire through the rearview mirror. "Will they be in the papers?"

Blaire shrugged. "Who knows? They're supposed to send a photographer at the end of the two weeks to take our picture. They asked me a few questions last night . . . kind of an interview, I guess. We'll probably end up in one of those supermarket tabloids, right alongside a story about Elvis living on Jupiter where he weighs next to nothing."

"Is your butler a nice fella?" Dex asked.

"He's real nice," Molly piped up.

"Dad, you ought to come inside and meet him," Blaire suggested. "After all, he's part of our property for the next two weeks."

Dex parked the car in front of Blaire's house. "Don't mind if I do. You've already met him, honey?" he asked Agatha.

"Yes, I've had the pleasure." Agatha released a throaty laugh and unfolded herself from the car. "I think you'll like him, Dex."

Blaire unlocked the door, wondering what would greet them. She just hoped he hadn't spent the morning rearranging everything in the place so that she'd trip over her own furniture.

The whole house smelled of lemon oil—except for the kitchen, which held the irresistible aroma of freshly baked bread. Furniture gleamed, crystal and glass sparkled, and the carpet looked as if someone had gone over it on hands and knees with a bristle brush.

Agatha and Dex stood just inside the front door and let their eyes take it all in. Their mouths hung open, then curved into twin smiles.

"Looks like you've got yourself a domestic, honey," Dex said, then kissed Blaire's cheek.

"Well, come on in." She waved impatiently. "Don't just stand there gaping. You two act as if my house has never been clean."

"Aw, honey, we don't mean to," her father said. A tall blond man with closely cropped hair and a broad face, wreathed with laugh lines, Dexter Thomlin wasn't one to veil his thoughts or feelings. Blaire regarded him with loving amusement. He had lived by his hunches, his instincts, and had made a nice living off them. His brown eyes, warm and shrewd, sized up the situation, then he craned his neck and tried to peek around the kitchen door. "Is he in there?" Dex asked, sotto voce.

"I imagine so." Blaire stepped around him and into the kitchen where Ruben was drizzling frosting over a baking tray of hot cross buns. "Someone wants to check you out, Ruben," she said, making her tone as dry as possible. "Ruben Crosscroft, this is my father Dexter Thomlin. He's a retired captain of the Miami Police Department. Dad, meet Ruben, butler *extraordinaire*."

"Put her there, pal," Dex said in his usual never-met-a-stranger manner. He had a big voice, befitting his barrel chest.

Ruben wiped his hands on his white apron and shook Dexter's hand, firmly, confidently, in the way Blaire knew Dexter admired. "Good to meet you, captain. Miami, you say? I lived there for a while."

"Lots of crime in Miami," Dex said.

"Is there? I didn't notice. It's a beautiful city."

Dex puffed out his chest. "Yeah, it is. Me and the missus live outside Jacksonville now. We talked about retiring to the Keys, but we wanted to be closer to Blaire and Molly, so we landed in a condo this side of Jacksonville. What's in the Keys, anyway, except tourists and artsy-fartsy people."

"Watch it, Dad," Blaire warned. "The missus and I happen to fall into that last category."

"Aw, honey." Dex held her in an affectionate headlock. Usually, this didn't embarrass her, but with Ruben looking on, she wanted to find a hole and crawl in it.

"Daddy, please," she begged, dislodging herself and adjusting the collar of her dress.

"You know what I mean by that," Dex said, oblivious to her being ill at ease. "I'm not talking about *real* artists, but those people who like to rub elbows with artists and those swishy types." Dex's glance skittered to Ruben, and Blaire knew her father was assessing the man to see if he perhaps fit that mold. "You like to cook, do you?"

"Yes, sir, and I like to eat." Ruben grinned—no, smirked. A man-to-man kind of smirk Blaire hadn't seen him use before. "A man has his appetites, right, captain?"

Dex winked knowingly and punched Ruben's shoulder. "You got that right, pal. I hear you're thinking of opening your own restaurant. Are you familiar with Tony's Garden in Miami?"

"Sure am. I know the chef there."

"Yeah? I know the owner. Tony and me go way back. His brother was the best friend I had on the force, but he . . ."

Blaire slipped around the corner to join her mother and daughter in the living room. Agatha was looking through an issue of *People* with Molly.

"God, some of the horrid outfits these actors wear!" Agatha shuddered, making Molly laugh.

"Ruben is playing Daddy like a violin," Blaire said, dropping onto the sofa beside Agatha. "The man is amazing."

"Your father?"

"No, Ruben. I don't trust him."

"Why not?" Agatha asked.

"He's too good-looking . . . too charming . . . too perfect."

"I like him," Molly said. "Mom, you don't trust anybody except me, Grand and Pops."

"That's not true," Blaire argued.

"Isn't it?" Agatha said, smiling at Molly as the child squirmed off the couch and went skipping toward the kitchen. "You used to be trusting, but no more. Ever since your marriage, you've closed yourself off from people, Blaire."

"Mother, that's not—"

"It *is* true. Even your daughter has noticed it."

Blaire crossed her arms and slumped into a pout. "Well, who wouldn't be jaded after living with Jimmy Jacobs?"

"Don't let him strip the goodness from you, Blaire."

Blaire looked at her mother, startled by Agatha's comment. "You think he's done that?"

"To a certain extent, yes. I know you've had a hard time of it, dear," Agatha said, her voice softening and a gentle smile surfacing to sparkle in her eyes. "Divorce cuts the heart out of a person, I'm sure, but it shouldn't be a permanent disability. You see a handsome gentleman like Ruben and you immediately look for ways to chop him off at his knees."

Blaire stood up, restless, agitated. "Do I, really? I don't want to be like that, Mother."

"Then start seeing with kind eyes, Blaire—the way you used to before Jimmy disillusioned you."

"Mother..." Blaire turned to study her mother's perfectly made-up face. Agatha took care of her skin, her figure. Vanity looked good on Agatha Thomlin. The argumentative streak died in Blaire, and she began to understand her mother's logic.

"Yes?" Agatha asked, her plucked brows arching just right.

"I'm glad you're my mother," Blaire said. She laughed when her mother's eyes misted. "Goodness, you're not going to cry over that, are you?"

"It's been a while since you've said that to me, dear. I'm relieved to know you're still happy with me."

"Wouldn't have any other mother," Blaire assured her, dropping to the sofa again to drape an arm around Agatha's shoulders. "I guess you're right about me being too closeted. Trust isn't necessarily a bad thing, I suppose. But I don't ever want to be as naive as I was with Jimmy."

"Don't worry. You won't be. You *couldn't* be. Naiveté is something you can't get back once you've let it go. Like virginity." She shifted to admire the room. "My, my. Your place practically gleams."

"Was it so bad before Ruben?"

"No, of course not. You're a fair housekeeper. Better than me, certainly. But you make good money, so why not hire help? Do you enjoy housework?"

"No. Never."

"Then why get all defensive about someone else doing it?"

"I'm not defensive," Blaire said, then realized she sounded it. "It's just weird having someone poking around." She glanced behind her, making sure the coast was clear before she continued in a near whisper. "When I got home yesterday from my errands, he'd not only picked up Molly's room, but mine, too! Everything was straightened . . . my clothes hung up, and my . . . well, dirty ones had been placed in the hamper. The sheets on my bed had even been changed!"

"What's your point?" Agatha fluffed her shoulder-length russet hair. It had been a shade of red ever since Blaire had been in high school. Before that, it had been as God intended, dark blond. But Blaire had agreed with her mother that the bottled color was an improvement. "So he cleaned your room. Big deal."

"It felt odd. You know, having someone in my bedroom touching my things." She shivered dramatically. "I think I'm going to tell him to stay out of there and to keep his hands off my clothing."

Widening her catlike eyes, Agatha made a tsk-tsking sound. "For pity's sake, Blaire, he's a butler, not a robber baron or a panty pervert."

"I know, but I think I'll—"

"Let him do his job," Agatha insisted, laying one hand on Blaire's, which were clasped tightly in her lap. "It's only for a couple of weeks, so live it up." She sat back, sprawling in feline laziness. "Your father's investigation of Ruben turned up some interesting things." Her green eyes twinkled. "Want to hear?"

Blaire chewed on her lower lip. She could hear her father's voice, punctuated occasionally by Ruben's attractive, deep-throated laugh and Molly's bubbling giggle. Burning to know more about her butler, she acquiesced with a shrug. "Tell me," she said, pulling her feet up on the sofa and snuggling into a comfortable position.

"He's never been married," Agatha said, smiling.

"I know. Maybe he doesn't like girls."

Agatha made a face and flapped one hand. "No way. You don't believe that for one minute." Her eyes sharpened. "Do you?"

Blaire wrinkled her nose. "No. When it comes to sex, he's into opposites."

Agatha nodded, emphatically. "He's been a chef in a few rather tony restaurants in London, New York, Miami, Fort Lauderdale and Palm Beach. Moves around quite a bit."

"Sounds like it."

"He's trained . . . schooled."

"Yes, I saw his diplomas."

"His last job was as a chef in Palm Beach. He quit a few weeks ago."

"Palm Beach," Blaire repeated. "Pricey neighborhood."

"Yes. Joe's Bar and Grill is definitely not his style."

Molly barreled into the living room, followed more sedately by Ruben, who was bearing a tray which he placed on the coffee table in front of the couch.

"Excuse me, but I thought you ladies might want a spot of tea. Please, sample my hot cross buns. They're fresh from the oven."

"I ate two," Molly announced, plopping onto the couch between Blaire and Agatha. "They're sweet and fluffy."

"Oh?" Agatha eyed Ruben speculatively, making Blaire cringe, because she knew a double entendre couldn't be far behind. Agatha reached for a bun and squeezed it, then tasted it with suggestive deliberation. "Delicious. I read somewhere that many women are first attracted to a man's buns." Agatha's gaze moved briefly from Ruben to Dexter standing behind him. She exchanged a look of mischief with her husband before her gaze eased back to the butler. "Using that criteria, Ruben, you are a *very* attractive man."

Blaire struggled not to blush, but she felt the heat scorch her cheeks. Her mother had always had a lusty sense of humor, shared and encouraged by her father, but she'd never been completely comfortable with it. Feeling awkward, she realized she was the only one in the room who wasn't laughing, so she forced a merry sound from her throat. Her timing was rotten. The other laughter had dwindled, lending hers an even phonier ring.

"It's so nice to have a man around the house," Agatha said, lifting the basket of rolls and offering them to Dex. "Especially one who cooks."

Blaire wondered if she should trust her impulse to let down her guard. Ruben would be in her life two weeks, so maybe she should simply relax and enjoy it. She gave a mental shrug, remembering her mother's advice about being more kindly. Ruben excused himself and started for the kitchen. Absently, Blaire reached for Ruben's buns while she admired the ones God had given him. Nice, she thought. *Very* nice.

GROCERY SHOPPING with Ruben was an experience. Normally, Blaire, armed with a list, could fly through the store and checkout stand within an hour. But not with Ruben in tow.

Her parents had offered to stay with Molly while Blaire had taken Ruben to the neighborhood grocery. The large store was busy for a Sunday afternoon. It's a good thing Molly isn't with us, Blaire thought, tapping her foot impatiently while Ruben examined each and every beef roast. Molly had no patience for shopping and would be begging to go home by now. In fact, Blaire wasn't far from begging herself.

"This one is nicely marbled," Ruben said to the butcher. "But I wonder if you might trim this outside fat to one-sixteenth of an inch?"

"Yes, sir. I can do that."

"And these pork chops . . ."

"Yes, sir?"

"Do you have any sliced a bit thinner?"

"No, but I can slice some up for you. How thick do you want them?"

"A fourth of an inch will do."

"Anything else?"

"Yes, could you run these three pounds of round through your grinder again?"

"Sure."

"Thanks so much."

Blaire shook her head. In all the years she'd gone to the grocery she'd never asked the butcher to do anything special for her. In fact, she couldn't remember even having a conversation with a grocery butcher. Glancing at her list, she decided to gather the items on it while Ruben made camp in front of the meat counter. In record time she harvested a bag of sugar, can of coffee, bottle of pancake syrup and two boxes of cereal and headed back to Ruben. He was still where she'd left him, but now he had a visitor.

An attractive woman in her fifties stood beside him, smiling into his face, her own features sculpted by professional hands and highlighted by artful makeup. Her glossy blond hair waved over her head. Her clothes were casual, but trendy. Her fingers sparkled with jewels. Blaire hung back, concealed behind a display of cake mixes. Cake mixes! She'd need one for Molly's birthday.

"So you're no longer with Earla?" the woman asked Ruben, and Blaire put aside thoughts of birthday cakes to listen to the conversation.

"That's right. I'm scouting the area for a good place to open my restaurant."

"Is Earla financing it?"

"No." That word came out ice-cold. Blaire could feel the chill in the air from where she stood.

"Well, if you need another backer, I might be tempted. Since Harry and I ended it all, I've found the beach house here far more charming than the main house in Palm Beach. In fact, I'm selling it. The only rub is I have to give Harry half of what I get for it. That's part of our divorce settlement." She laid a hand on his sleeve. "So don't be a stranger, Ruben. Harry left me well-off, the old skinflint, and I could be persuaded to throw a little money your way if you sweetened the deal just right."

"That's nice of you, Julia, but I believe I have sufficient funds."

"Think about it. I always thought Earla was lucky to have you. I still can't believe she gave you up."

"It was a mutual parting of the ways."

Julia laughed and leaned close to him to add in a lower tone, "Parting of the sheets, you mean."

Julia laughed again. Ruben didn't. The butcher handed Ruben the paper-wrapped parcels, and Ruben turned his attention to the meat purchases again.

"Good to see you, Julia," he said, effectively dismissing her. "Got to dash off, don't you know."

"Yes, and I must round up Bessie. You know where my beach house is?"

"I remember."

"Here . . ." She tucked a card into his jacket pocket. "This has my phone number on it. Call me sometime."

Blaire rounded her shoulders, making herself smaller as Ruben turned and glanced around. He dumped the meat packages into the shopping cart, then set off for the fresh seafood section. Julia walked briskly past Blaire, tossing her a haughty glance. Blaire eyed the woman, wondering if she talked that way to every man she met or if Ruben was special. An uneasiness stirred in Blaire as she dissected the overheard conversation. The woman—Julia—had propositioned Ruben. She'd all but told him she'd give him money if he came around to visit her. Like a hired stud or something.

Shaking her head, Blaire told herself she was jumping to damning conclusions again, another example of her distrustfulness of the general population. The two *could* be old friends and the suggestiveness of the conversation just light banter between two people who went way, way back. Why, her very own mother was guilty of such double entendre on any given day, and Agatha Thomlin was *never* serious. Agatha flirted and insinuated and remained steadfastly faithful to her Sexy Dexy.

Just playful patter, Blaire told herself, inching around her blind and strolling toward Ruben, her arms full of items. She dropped her selections in the cart, and he whirled around from his minute study of packaged red snapper.

"There you are!" He surveyed the things she'd thrown into the cart. "Am I dawdling too long?"

Blaire checked over her list. "Let's just say, I've seen tortoises move faster."

"Are we in a hurry?"

"No, but I'm sure Mother and Dad would like to head back to Jacksonville soon." She glanced to the place where she'd been hidden. "What kind of cake mix do you think Molly would like best? Spice or devil's food?"

"Mix? I've hardly ever used a mix. Couldn't I whip one up from scratch?"

"From scratch." She should have known.

"I make a double chocolate royale that always receives high praise. It would be a perfect birthday cake."

"Sounds good. Molly loves chocolate."

"I'll need a few items . . . butter—"

"I have margarine on my list." She noted his slight frown and added, "But I can get some butter, too."

"Good, and some fresh whipping cream and blocks of chocolate . . . oh, and cherries for the garnish."

Blaire motioned for him to precede. "Just get what you need."

"Have you candles?"

"Yes, those I already have. Regular twisty birthday candles in pastel colors are all right with you, aren't they?"

"Of course. Do you like snapper?"

"Yes, sometimes. Actually, Molly and I aren't too keen on seafood. I know that's weird, being from Florida and everything, but most fish turns our stomachs. Snapper and grouper we can tolerate. But no lobster or shrimp, please."

"Oysters?"

She made a gagging sound.

"Clams?"

She rolled her eyes and gulped.

"Crayfish, dolphin, octopus, swordfish, shark." He laughed at the face she made with each suggestion. "Okay, we'll stick with red meat and chicken. It's all right with me. I've gotten weary of seafood lately. I'm just as happy with beef and pork."

Blaire fell into step beside him as they headed for the dairy refrigerators. The section gave a clear view of the checkout islands. Julia stood near one and waved at Ruben.

"Ruben, that woman is waving at you, I think," Blaire said, watching him carefully for his reaction.

He looked at Julia, furrowed his brow and essayed a short, halfhearted wave in response. He paled, looking a bit green around the gills.

"A friend of yours?" Blaire asked.

"Not really." He returned his attention to steering the cart. Blaire had to almost trot to catch up with him.

"You know her, though," Blaire persisted. *Don't lie to me*, she told him, silently. *Just tell the truth. Pretty please?*

"I helped her select a good roast," he said, then pointed down an aisle. "There are the bottled cherries. Let me grab a few more items and I'll be done. I'm not stretching your budget, am I? I'm trying to get only the necessities."

"No, you're not stretching my budget." *Just my patience. You lied. How am I supposed to trust people when they lie to me right and left?* She commandeered the cart. "I'll go ahead and start checking out while you finish up."

"Okay. I'll be right with you."

She watched sadly, as he strode toward the baking aisle. He's covering up his past, she thought. But why? Must be a checkered one. Maybe he *is* a hired stud. She laughed at that. How ridiculous! Still . . . wonder who Earla is? Would he lie about her, too?

Julia waited near the automatic doors while the sack boy sorted and packed her groceries. A dour-faced black woman stood beside her. Bessie, her domestic? Blaire wondered. Her gaze wandered to the last few items the boy was sorting. A pot roast disappeared into the paper sack. Roast. So, she *did* buy one. Ruben told a white lie instead of a black one, Blaire thought, giving him his due.

She noted, however, that Ruben didn't join her at the checkout island until Julia and her employee had left the building.

4

"LET'S PLAY AGAIN," Molly said, beginning to set up the Clue game board again.

"No, I'm shagged out," Blaire begged off. "Time for you to hit the sack, sprout."

"It's early."

"Past nine," Blaire said, glancing at the digital clock in her video player. "It's Sunday night, and you have school tomorrow, Molly."

Molly made a face, but packed away the game. "How come Ruben stayed in his room tonight?"

"Because he's a nice guy. He understands that you and I are used to being alone with each other. Molly, he's not a guest. He's supposed to be working for us."

"I know, but I like him and I want him to like us."

"He does. He's probably used to being by himself and prefers it." Oh, what a pretty lie, Blaire thought, knowing that a man who looked like Ruben didn't spend too many nights alone. She patted Molly's behind. "Give me a hug." She held Molly to her for a sweet moment. "Good night, kiddo. Love you."

"Love you, too." Molly grabbed her favorite stuffed bear and toddled off to bed.

When she heard Molly's bedroom door close, Blaire kicked off her tennis shoes and stretched out on the sofa. She closed her eyes and let her bones liquefy.

What a day! Agatha and Dex had stayed to share a light dinner of ham-and-cheese omelets, croissants and iced tea, prepared by Ruben. They'd left for Jacksonville just before sundown. Blaire sighed, enjoying the time she'd finally found for herself. She'd grown used to living alone with only Molly's welfare placed before her own. She thought ahead to Jimmy's impending visit and dreaded it. Of course, he most likely wouldn't show up for Molly's birthday. Jimmy's promises were about as solid as California's fault lines.

She wondered if Jimmy had changed, but doubted it. That had been her biggest mistake; thinking he'd change once they were married. She'd suspected all the time she dated him that his roving eye sometimes led him down an unfaithful path, yet her foolish heart had convinced her that he'd take marriage vows seriously. But Jimmy's heart had never been in the marriage. Courting was his forte. Marriage confounded him. He just couldn't get a handle on fidelity.

After seven years of marriage and one child, Blaire had thrown in the towel. Jimmy hadn't wanted the divorce. He'd promised never to sleep around again, but he'd made that promise before. His fooling around with other women had placed Blaire into a role she hadn't liked—that of the long-suffering wife. She'd filed for divorce while she'd still had her pride and dignity intact.

The sound of running water shook Blaire from her reverie, and she sat up. Listening intently as fear scratched her throat, she pictured the baseball bat propped near the front door and wondered if she should make a dash for it. Wait . . . it's the shower. What burglar takes a shower before he lifts your jewels? It's the butler, dummy. Laughing at herself, she fell back on the couch.

He's keeping to his promised schedule, she noted, recalling his agreement to shower in the evenings and not interfere with her or Molly's morning rituals.

Wonder what he did in his room all evening? she mused. Wonder what he looks like in his all-together?

She groaned. Heaven help her, she sounded just like her mother! She needed to get out and socialize, she told herself. When a woman resorted to fantasizing about her butler in the shower, it was time for her to go a-hunting.

She vaguely remembered fantasizing about Jimmy when they'd first met back in college, but her dreams had been much better than the real thing. As Agatha Thomlin would say, Jimmy Jacobs had a tendency to misfire and was, more often than not, too quick on the draw.

The nice thing about having a husband who made love like he ran track—finishing first was his only objective—was that Blaire didn't pine for a man's company at night after her divorce. In fact, it was a relief not to worry about where Jimmy was sleeping and who he was sleeping with and if that someone practiced safe sex.

Since the divorce three years ago, she hadn't been lonely because she had Molly, and she hadn't been financially strapped because she'd worked all through her marriage and had earned contracts from a major publisher before her marriage had ended. Granted, she'd been so busy keeping the bills paid and providing a good life for her daughter that she'd had little or no time for a social calendar, but there were worse things in life.

Blaire frowned, sensing the false ring to that last thought. Her busy schedule really had nothing to do with the lack of romance in her life. She'd thrown herself into motherhood and being a good breadwinner because she was scared. Simply scared.

Having her romantic dreams ground to dust had led to insecurity and cowardice. Her few evenings out had proved one thing to her—she wasn't a fit companion for a man. She was too uptight, too quick to find fault, too frightened to be herself and enjoy the moment. She'd told herself it was too soon, that in time she'd regain her self-confidence and throw her heart into the ring again.

But it seemed she'd become insulated, and she knew it wasn't good for her to hold herself away from men. Deep down, she wanted to be involved with someone. Lately, she'd even been eager to build a fire in a man's eyes again. The right man, she added. She had Molly to think of this time around. Above all, she wanted the next man in her life to be a good father to her daughter.

A delicious aroma teased her nostrils and triggered a spiraling sensation in her stomach. Ruben, she thought, sniffing the tantalizing scent of his after-shave. Her other senses fell into line, alerting her to Ruben's proximity. It's not Old Spice, she thought, which was her father's preference. It's not Brüt, either, which is what Jimmy had taken baths in. She sensed Ruben's surprise at seeing her, his retreat, and she opened her eyes.

"Ruben?" she called before he could duck out of the living room.

"Yes?" Worry flitted across his face. "I'm sorry if I awakened you."

"No...I wasn't..." Her voice deserted her as her gaze flitted nervously over him.

Khaki-colored running shorts and a tight-fitting tank top hugged him, showcased him. Body hair darkened his copper-tinted skin. Droplets sparkled in the hair on his head.

He has a hiker's body, she thought. She could picture him striding up a hillside and thrashing through undergrowth. Her gaze lingered on a long scar running alongside his left kneecap.

"I don't want to bother you," he said, turning to go. "I was about to brew a pot of tea, but I can do without."

"No, don't..." She'd stopped shy of begging him to keep her company. "That is, tea sounds nice. I wouldn't mind having a cup myself."

"You'd join me?"

"Sure." She hitched herself up to a sitting position. "I'd even spring for some chocolate-chip cookies. They're in the jar beside the refrigerator."

He pointed at her, pistol-style. "Gotcha. Be back in a sec."

Blaire followed him with her eyes. "Ruben?"

"Yes?" he asked, pausing just behind her.

"What's the name of that after-shave you're wearing?"

"Is it a bit much?"

"No. I like it. What's it called?"

"Bold Hunter, I believe. It's new on the market."

"Smells good." From the corner of her eye she saw him give a quick smile before resuming his trip to the kitchen.

Blaire listened to water rushing into the kettle and the tinkle of china. Bold Hunter. Well, he probably could live up to that name if he put his mind to it, she thought, warming to the idea. He probably had some slick moves. It was easy to imagine him as a sleek, dark jungle cat. She had a feeling he wasn't as easygoing as he tried to appear. He's temperamental, she surmised. He's probably a demanding chef, a perfectionist at work. Less than the best wouldn't be his style.

He brought the tray in and set it on the coffee table, then poured the steaming tea from the pot into delicate china cups.

"Tell me about being a chef," she said, genuinely curious about him. "Is there a lot of stress?"

"Sometimes. It requires stamina and meticulous planning. You don't just walk in and start cooking. You must plan your menus in advance, select your produce and meat, and then arrange your utensils." He flashed her an apologetic smile. "But you know that. Most women do."

"Well, I'm not most women. The kitchen has never held much appeal to me. I'm hoping Molly will take to it, but the prospects are dim."

"I've always loved it. Cooking for the public, of course, is different. The top restaurants view their menus as an art form. Each dish must be an experience to treasure. It's up to the chef to make it so."

"The restaurant takes on the personality of the chef?" Blaire asked.

He nodded while adding two lumps of sugar to his steaming cup of tea. His large hands seemed to swallow up the cup and saucer. Blaire found herself watching his hands, caught by the contrast of their size and their gentleness. Leashed strength, she fancied. Like a stallion haltered by a rope or a jungle cat sheathing its murderous claws.

"It's gratifying when people follow you from restaurant to restaurant," he said, breaking into her thoughts. "That's when you know you've carved out a niche."

Ruben went to the patio door and opened it a few inches. Tipping back his head, he enjoyed the touch of the sea breeze on his face and neck. Blaire's watchful regard was having an effect on him. A tightness invaded his chest and loins and he shifted from foot to foot. What did she want from him? he wondered. More importantly, what did he want from her?

One glance assured him that she was still gazing at him, probing him with those catlike eyes of hers. He noticed that her eyes resembled Agatha's—olive green with flecks of gold at the centers. Her intense scrutiny was like waving a red flag at him and asking him to charge, but he wondered if she knew it. Somehow, he sensed she was naive, but that didn't make sense. She'd been married and divorced several years. She was no babe in the woods. But the feeling persisted, and a cautionary feeling ran through him, urging him to go slow and not take this woman lightly. He heeded the insight, since it had served him well over the years. More often than not, he'd known how to handle women and when to handle them.

He cleared his throat. "I love the ocean. I'm happier when I'm near it. Have you always lived in Florida?"

"Yes. Always."

"Always. That's a good word." He looked directly at her, and strong emotion pushed at his heart. What a beauty, he thought, taking in the tumble of her blond hair that framed a heart-shaped face. *You'd be so nice to come home to,* he hummed to himself. "I don't have 'always' in my life, but I want to. Always. Feels good just to say it."

Transfixed, she continued to stare at him. Where had this poet, this romantic, come from? What happened to that jungle cat? He's complex, she thought. Much more complicated than she'd judged him to be.

"I've been a gypsy wanderer." He sighed, his chest rising and falling impressively. "But my inner clock tells me it's time to pitch my tent permanently."

"You might miss traveling, having no ties."

"Maybe, but I'd like to try it and see."

Blaire sat all the way up to fully appreciate the moonlight shimmering across the dark waves of his hair. He shifted his weight to one bare foot. The movement held a measure of masculine grace. Studying him as she would a statue in a museum, she took pleasure from his body: in the delineation of muscle, the lankiness of limb, the sturdy strength of his frame.

A gypsy wanderer longing for roots. What a nice image, she thought. But would he really like being tied down to one place or to one woman? Chances were good that he'd find his bounds too confining. Like Jimmy, who had never been able to stay put for long.

"So, you don't share Molly's interest in contests?"

"No. I'm a skeptic about things like that. Lotteries, games of chance, lucky numbers." She wrinkled her nose, dismissing them.

"But no more." His eyes slid in her direction briefly. "I'm here to make a believer out of you."

Oh, I believe . . . I believe you are one magnificent-looking man, she thought, then blinked hard. Her eyes watered as if she'd been staring at the sun.

"How long were you married?"

"Seven years," she answered automatically. "Divorced three. I was just thinking about that before you came in. I can't believe it's been so long." She laughed, but didn't feel like it. "Time slipped by when I wasn't looking."

"It has a way of doing that."

She saw the glint of gold amid the hairs on his chest. "That necklace . . . is it a religious medallion?"

"No." He fingered it absently. "It's a gold coin taken from a shipwreck off the coast of Jamaica. I was the cook for the salvage team."

"That sounds exciting."

"It was, but I was glad to see land again. We were at sea for six weeks. Six weeks of water, water, everywhere and not a woman in sight. That was grim." His full-lipped mouth thinned. "Bloody grim."

Her study of him took a different tack. She imagined him sex-starved after weeks at sea. Her pulse pounded, prodded by the fantasy of having him make love to her in a wild frenzy. "Do you have a lady somewhere?"

"A . . . lady?" His brows lowered, forming a straight line above his eyes. "Oh, you mean, am I sleeping with someone?"

"No, I didn't say that . . . I wouldn't." She puffed out a breath. Talk about direct! This guy came right at you! "That's none of my business."

He shrugged. "Sorry if I embarrassed you."

"You didn't. I'm just . . . you assumed I was getting personal."

"Weren't you?"

"No." She waved a hand at him. "Forget it." Shouldn't have asked him about that, anyway. Who he slept with—*saw socially*—wasn't anything to her. Just like a man to think she was asking about his sex life. "Some people still just date, you know," she said, under her breath, but he heard her.

He slid the door shut and leaned one shoulder against the wall. "Is that so?" he asked, clearly making fun of her. "Fancy that. Dating. What a quaint idea."

"Oh, put a very British sock in it."

He chuckled and lowered one lid in a sexy wink. "You win." The devil's lights dimmed in his eyes. "Blaire, it's been quite awhile since I was anyone's domestic, and I never much cared for the job. I'm doing this strictly for the money. I'm not your stereotypical butler—wooden, unfeeling, sexless. I'm a man. You're a woman."

Blaire swallowed the lump beginning to form in her throat. "What are you getting at?"

"Let's be friends, not just butler and lady of the manor. Getting to know each other will be fun. It is already." He poured himself another cup of tea while he ticked off a list. "Your favorite color is red. Your favorite perfume is Vanderbilt. Your favorite fabric is cotton, and you like big band music. You're a borderline vegetarian because veggies are easy to prepare. You're great at—"

"Wait, wait...hold it just one minute!" Blaire set her cup and saucer down. "How'd you know all that? Who have you been talking to? My Mother? My Dad? Molly?" She narrowed her eyes suspiciously.

"Hardly." He said the word with equal measures of ridicule and affront. "I'm observant, that's all. Haven't you noticed anything about me?"

"No. I have better things to do than—"

"You noticed my after-shave."

She snapped her jaws shut and glared at him. He'd just called her a liar, and she couldn't even upbraid him for it because he was right, damn him.

"You noticed my necklace, too."

"Okay, so I noticed a couple of things about you. Big deal." She eyed him curiously. "You want to be friends, buddies?" Somehow this didn't appeal to her. Never had mere friendship sounded so bland.

He sat on the edge of the recliner near her. "Blaire, you're special. I can see that. I want you to feel comfortable around me. I want you to feel you've made the right decision in letting me stay here."

"Are you buttering me up?"

"Maybe," he admitted, thinking it was becoming a habit, and one he should probably break, especially around Blaire. Even now she was regarding him guardedly.

"I've always heard that Australian men are manipulative, macho and cocky as hell."

He sat back, stunned by her assessment, then amused by her forthrightness. He grinned and decided to give her tit for tat. "And I've always heard that American women are self-centered, nagging ball-busters, but I'd never presume to lump them all into a string of nasty adjectives."

Blaire tried to beat him senseless with her hard glare. It didn't work. She shrugged, giving him the point.

"So what say we drop the servant-and-mistress routine. I like you. Don't you like me?"

"Well, yes, of course."

"After two weeks I'll probably still be in the area," he explained. "I think this is the right place for my restaurant, and there's no reason why we couldn't see each other."

"S-see each other?" Disbelief hammered her. What had brought this on? Here she was trying to get used to him being her butler and he was jumping ahead to—to what, exactly? "Date, you mean?"

"Sure." He swallowed hard. "Date." The word sounded phony coming from him. "Yeah, I could go for that. For starters."

Blaire studied him carefully, sensing that he didn't date women; he had affairs with them. His gaze lingered in all the right places, and she resisted the urge to cross her arms over her breasts. As the silence between them lengthened, Blaire grew self-conscious. She laughed, trying to break through the sexual tension that seemed nearly tangible.

He cradled his chin in one hand, never taking his gaze from her face. "You've got a great laugh there, Blaire. It's sultry, smoky, a little naughty."

"Oh, please." She snickered, desperate not to believe a word of it. "There you go spreading on the butter again." Nerves jangling, she reached for the teapot, but managed to tip over the cream pitcher. Milk flew in streams and droplets. Most of it landed on the front of Ruben's shorts. "Oh, great. Here . . . let me."

Blaire grabbed a napkin off the tray and dabbed at the wet spots. She rubbed harder, gathering the material in one hand while she scrubbed with the other.

"It's okay, Blaire."

"Thank heavens it wasn't the tea. That would have burned."

"Blaire . . . Blaire . . ." Self-consciousness colored his laughter. "Stop before I beg for more."

That's when Blaire's hand passed over a bump. No, a ridge. Something that hadn't been there a few moments ago. Or, rather, it hadn't been in that position a few moments ago. Blaire dropped the napkin and straightened up sharply. Heat engulfed her, sent her temperature soaring. She'd practically been fondling him, and from the look on his face, he'd enjoyed it!

"I'm sorry," Blaire mumbled. Her tongue felt like a leather flap in her mouth. "I didn't mean to . . . I wasn't thinking about—"

"No harm done," he said, his tone lower, huskier. He looked down at the wet spot on his fly. "You were just trying to butter me up."

"I was not!" Blaire noted the gleam in his eyes and felt her color rise again. Stupid to be talking about spilled milk when it wasn't what had them flustered, red-faced, breathless.

"Let me pour you another cup of tea."

"No, don't bother." She tried to breathe normally, but the air was hot, sexually charged. "I'm going to bed . . . to sleep." Her sense of humor rode to her rescue and she laughed. "I embarrassed myself," she admitted, glad that he was laughing, too.

"So did I." He glanced down at himself and shrugged helplessly. "It happens."

"Well, you certainly aren't a wooden, sexless butler."

"So glad you noticed."

She only had a moment to register the dark intent in his eyes and then a blur of movement. The shock of his mouth on hers made her stumble, retreat, hold out one hand in a defensive gesture. He caught her hand in his and brought it around to the middle of his back. Thoughts of resisting melted under the warmth of his lips and the sliding seduction of his tongue. Blaire flattened her hands against his back, let them roam and discover the muscled contours. His lips nibbled at hers, and then his tongue played suitor, teasing the inside of her mouth, mating with her own tongue. A mewling sound worked up Blaire's throat as she drove her fingers through his silky hair and held him fast. Her body arched against his. She moaned again when his hands cupped her buttocks to pull her intimately against his arousal. God, it had been so long since she'd wanted a man—*really* wanted someone. Her skin tingled from head to toe in delicious anticipation.

Bold hunter, she thought, rattled and shaken to her soul. Desire, hot and searing, blazed through her, and she broke away from him. His chest lifted and fell with his ragged breathing. Blaire could feel her own lungs expand and contract. Seconds sizzled between them, and nearly a full minute passed before Blaire braved speech.

"Please, I don't . . . I can't . . ."

His smile disarmed her, gentled her. "I understand." He ran a hand through his hair, mussing it further. "We got a bit carried away. Well, look . . . it happens to everyone now and then."

"Does it?" She blinked, realizing too late that she'd revealed more than she'd intended. "I mean, right. Happens to everyone. Well . . ." She glanced around, looking for an escape hatch. "Guess I'll turn in. 'Night, Ruben." She hurried from the room, head down, body tense, pastel pink lingering on her cheeks.

Ruben carried the tea tray into the kitchen and washed and rinsed the dishes, giving his body time to return to normal. The woman had certainly gone to his head. He'd meant to test her waters, but he'd taken a plunge, knocked completely off balance by Blaire's hidden delights. The way her hands had caressed his back and shoulders—and then she'd raked her fingers through his hair in a wanton display of passion that had sent him into a swan dive. Things were moving so fast he couldn't keep up. His plan early on was to take the money, do the job and clear out fast. But that had been before he'd seen Blaire, before he'd wanted Blaire, before he'd tasted Blaire. He knew one thing for sure. He wanted more. Much, much more.

You're lucky, mate, he told himself. She could have been a prune-faced shrew with a flock of shrieking children and a beer-swilling slob for a husband. But you've struck it rich!

He strolled back into the living room and out the patio door into the night, the smell of the ocean luring him. All the comforts of home, he thought, looking at the house, the swing set and the patio furniture. Oddly, he did feel comfortable.

Don't dig in too far, he cautioned himself. He knew instinctively that Blaire Thomlin, mother and career woman, wouldn't approve of his past employment. Hell, he didn't even approve of it. It had merely been the quickest way he knew of to get the money he needed to open his own restaurant and be his own boss. And there had only been two women—three counting Earla—acquaintances who had insisted on paying him for doing them favors like taking them to functions because they didn't want to go alone. Earla had hired him as chef at one of her restaurants, and one thing had led to another. She'd paid him twice what he was worth as a chef, but he'd earned the pay in other ways. At first it had been fun, affectionate, but then things had soured. He closed himself off from the memories and the mistakes.

Maybe, just maybe, Blaire might overlook his past once she got to know him better. But it would take some time. Some women were excited by the idea of a man sought after for his sexual savoir faire, but Blaire wasn't one of them.

Two weeks. Not much time, mate. Then he grinned and sauntered into the house. Luckily, he was at his best under pressure.

5

BLAIRE NIBBLED ON the last of the ham-and-cheese-stuffed croissant Ruben had prepared for her lunch. She pulled back the protective sheets on the drawing of a lop-eared rabbit she'd been touching up and decided it was finished. She knew she could keep adding and refining and shading until doomsday, but she also knew that perfectionism didn't pay the rent. Her deadline was days away, and she had to meet it.

She glanced at the clock, pleased to see that it was only twelve-thirty. She'd gotten quite a bit done that morning on her illustrations for a children's book about Donner Rabbit and his forest friends. After a quick breakfast prepared by Ruben, she'd retired to her office and hadn't been interrupted until Ruben had brought her lunch. She'd taken time to admire his choice of snug black jeans and a gray, pin-striped shirt. Looking at him, she'd had an urge to pinch herself because she must be dreaming. Winning a husky butler for two whole weeks was too good to be true.

He'd even fixed a hearty breakfast and packed a nutritious lunch for Molly to take to school. Earlier, Blaire had heard the washer start and had assumed he was doing the laundry. Trepidation wiggled up her spine when she thought of him sorting her lacy bras and bikini panties. Dumb to get all weird about that stuff, she knew, but she couldn't quite dispel the image or the uneasiness. It wouldn't be so bad if Ruben was a dotty old gent. Who'd care if he admired her bras and other undies? But Ruben was virile, sexy and single, and he was up close and personal with her personals.

Her trip with him yesterday to the grocery store invaded her mind and made her frown. Her instincts told her that he hadn't been completely truthful about that woman he'd been talking to in front of the meat counter. They knew each other. The woman had mentioned someone named Earla. Why didn't Ruben want to admit knowing her? Why was he being so mysterious about his life?

Drinking the last of her iced tea, she slipped off the high stool and set the lunch tray near the door. She stretched bunched muscles and bent over to touch her toes. The phone rang, but she ignored it, knowing that Ruben would intercept the call as he'd done twice that morning. Wonderful to have a live answering service, she thought, then cautioned herself not to get too used to the luxury. *He's only yours temporarily, then you'll have to rough it again. To think she'd been reluctant to accept Molly's winnings!*

The phone kept ringing...five, six, seven...where's Ruben? Blaire glanced out the window and saw flapping sheets on the line. Ruben stepped into view to fasten clothespins to them. Blaire snatched up the phone receiver in the middle of the tenth ring.

"Hello?"

"Yes, finally." The woman's voice was cigarette-roughened and smoky with disdain. "Ruben Crosscroft, if you please."

"Just a moment." Blaire started to put down the receiver, but the caller had pricked her curiosity. "Who shall I say is calling?" she asked, using her own version of cool disdain.

"Tell Ruben it's Earla Nivens."

Blaire felt her eyes widen. *Earla!* She swallowed and forced herself to speak in a normal voice. "Please hold." Blaire laid the receiver beside the phone and went to the patio door. "Ruben," she called, and he poked his head around a snapping sheet. "Telephone for you."

"For me?" He leaped over the laundry basket and bounded toward her, clearly surprised. "Is it the contest people?"

"No." Blaire waited until he was right up to her and she could see every nuance. "Earla Nivens?" she said, making it an inquiry and hoping he'd enlighten her.

His surprise dissolved into irritation. Lines appeared between his eyes and at the corners of his wide mouth. "Oh. Thanks." The answer was short and hardly revealing.

Blaire stepped aside to let him in. He reminded her of a bull, head down and charging.

"I'll take it in the kitchen," he said.

"Right. I'll hang up the extension in my study," Blaire said, moving in that direction. She ached to listen in, but she made herself replace the receiver. Somehow, she knew that Ruben wouldn't say a word, anyway, until he heard the click, signaling it was no longer a "party line."

Blaire sauntered toward the studio door, closing it slowly as she cocked an ear. She could hear Ruben's voice, but she couldn't make out a word of the conversation.

"Drat." She shut the door, admitting defeat. Earla Nivens. What a name. What kind of woman went along with it? Her voice had held a note of cultured boredom, often found in wealthy women. She'd said Ruben's name as if she was very familiar with it. Ruben must have given her this number, so why had he seemed so miffed when Earla Nivens had used it? Maybe that had been an act for Blaire's benefit. Maybe he was, at this very moment, telling Earla how *glad* he was to hear from her.

Thanks for calling, he was probably saying to Earla Nivens. This place is such a bore and Blaire Thomlin is . . . well, she isn't you. It's so great to hear your voice. Can't wait until this is over and we can be together again.

Blaire realized she was staring gloomily out the window and working on a doozy of a depression. She heard the sliding door open and close, and then Ruben came into view outside. He lifted one of Molly's T-shirts from the basket, shook it out violently, and pegged it to the line, his movements abrupt, angry.

Switching off the table lamp, Blaire moved with purpose to the patio door. She pushed it aside and stood on the threshold. The April breeze off the ocean was brisk, flapping the clothes on the line and making them billow like sails. Ruben turned and noticed her. He lifted one dark brow, asking a silent question. The simple gesture made Blaire suck in a breath. Heavens, he was good on the eyes! When movie-star-handsome features had been passed out, Ruben had been first in line. She told herself not to be nosy, but curiosity overruled her caution.

"Is she your girlfriend?" she asked, barging right in, nose first.

"Who?" He acted dumb for a second, then gave up. Dumb was a poor fit on him. "No. Earla's just a friend."

"Calling to see how you're doing?" Blaire persisted. Damn him, he was going to tell her something if she had to drag it out of him.

"Sort of. I told her not to call here again."

Blaire lifted a careless hand. "Why? I don't mind. You gave her my number, so you must have figured she'd use it."

"I didn't give her this number," he said, shaking out a pair of jeans before hanging them on the line. "She called Silent Butler and they gave her your number. Sorry."

"No problem."

"Anyway, she said she wouldn't call again."

"Like I said, no problem." She sauntered toward him. "I have a dryer, you know."

"I know, but I saw this clothesline and I decided it would be best. I love the smell of sunshine in linens and towels. I dried the delicates in the dryer already. Thought I'd clean the windows next."

"You don't have to . . ." She bit off the rest. Let him do things, she told herself. He's your butler, not your guest. "Okay. If you want. Lord knows they need it. I can't remember the last time I washed them inside and out."

"It gives me a good excuse to be outside where I can smell the ocean."

"You could take some time off and go to the beach. I won't dock your pay."

He grinned at her from around a pair of Molly's jeans. "Actually, I've already been to the beach today. I got up at five and went jogging. The sunrise was spectacular."

"Do you always beat the sun up or did you have trouble sleeping?"

"I like mornings."

She made a face. "Not me."

"I like evenings, too, if the book is well written or the company's good." He hung a pair of her denim shorts on the line. Skimpy, short shorts. "I'd like to see you in these." He glanced at her in time to see her blush. "Blaire, about last night . . ."

"Nothing happened," she said, heading him off. "You make it sound as if we made love on the coffee table."

His mouth twisted as he struggled to keep from laughing. He ran a hand down his face, pulling a serious expression. "I don't mean to harp on this, but you seem so edgy today. If I offended you, I—"

"You didn't," she said, too quickly. "Believe it or not, I've been kissed before." She made a throwaway gesture. "I didn't expect it, that's all. After my Mrs. Clean act, I was off balance and embarrassed, and, well, the kiss didn't help me regain my equilibrium." Why was she rattling on? The man hadn't asked for a color commentary. "Let's forget it, okay?"

"Yes, of course. I wasn't complaining, but I can certainly understand your not enjoying being kissed by me."

"I didn't say I didn't enjoy being—" She cut short that admission, realizing she was stepping into an age-old trap. Squinting against the sun at him, she noted the glint of humor in his blue eyes. "All right, Ruben. I'm on to your game, pal. You want some strokes? Okay, here goes." She clasped her hands in ecstasy. "You made the earth move under my feet. Angels were singing, my heart went winging, and I felt like a-ding-a-linging."

His burst of laughter triggered her own. The shared merriment erased the leftover tension from last night. Dimples played in his lean cheeks as he laughed, and Blaire admired her prize. Finally, she forced herself to move away from his seductive presence.

"Having recited my poem, I'll leave you to admire it."

"Hey, where are you going?" He sounded disappointed.

"I've got some errands to run."

"How about taking a walk on the beach with me first? You've been working all morning and some of the afternoon. You deserve a little break, don't you?"

"Well, I . . ." She gazed into the distance, hearing the cry of sea gulls. Walking along the white sand with Ruben seemed like heaven. "My errands can wait a few minutes. I do deserve a break."

"Me, too. You're lucky to live so near the beach." He angled his elbow toward her and arched a brow. "Shall we?"

Blaire hesitated before taking his arm and strolling beside him to the beach. Over the rise they stopped to kick off their shoes and walk barefoot on the warm, sugary sand. Terns pecked and poked for snacks along the shore, and gulls and pelicans sailed overhead. In the dim distance a ship bobbed on the watery horizon.

"I am lucky," Blaire agreed. "It's always beautiful here. Even in the dead of winter."

"Did you ever want to leave it? Florida, I mean."

"Not really. I went to college nearby and I earned a degree in art. After graduation I was offered a job in Kansas City, Missouri, as an artist for a greeting card company. That was the only time I seriously considered moving."

"But you didn't?"

"No, for several reasons. First and foremost, I also received an offer from a publisher to do illustrations for a book on flowers. I decided to be my own boss and try to make it as a free-lance artist."

"And you made the right decision, I'd say. You seem to be doing quite well for yourself."

"I can't complain." She'd become increasingly aware of their bodies rubbing against each other as they walked. He stood several inches taller than her, but she noticed that he shortened his stride to accommodate her. She stumbled, and he placed his hand over hers. Blaire smiled at him, wondering if he felt the same intimacy that curled through her like smoke.

"What were your other reasons for not moving away?"

"My reasons... oh, yes." She got back on track. "Well, Jimmy, my then husband, was away a lot, and I didn't want to be alone in a strange city. Also, I was pregnant. I knew my doctor here, and I was familiar with the hospital... my parents were here. So, I decided to stay put."

"Was your husband playing football then?" He noted her startled glance. "Molly told me he played."

"Yes, he did. He hasn't been with a team in quite a few years. He was a college standout, but he sustained injuries in his first pro season and never fully recovered."

"Rotten luck."

"It wasn't all bad. The first team had to pay out his contract no matter what, so he did fine financially."

"What's he doing now?"

"I'm not sure. He does a lot of odd jobs. Jimmy doesn't stay in places long. He's worked in sporting goods stores, done commercials, been on speech circuits, dabbled in all sorts of get-rich-quick schemes."

"Did you work during your marriage?"

"Yes, thank God. When we divorced, I was self-sufficient."

"So Jimmy will be here for Molly's birthday?"

"He says so, but he might not show. He's like that. He has good intentions, but rarely follows through." She realized the conversation was one-sided and decided to change that. "Does Earla live near here?"

He jerked his head around to face her. "Earla?"

"Yes, the woman who called you."

"Uh . . . no. She lives in Palm Beach."

"That's where you worked before you came here?"

"Yes, I worked for her. She owns restaurants in Palm Beach, St. Petersburg and Miami."

"Is that other woman in the restaurant business, too?"

"What other woman?" he asked, lowering his brows.

"The one in the grocery. The one you helped select a roast." She pulled her hand from beneath his with the pretense of picking up a chipped sand dollar. She examined it, but felt his gaze burn the top of her bent head. Blaire lifted her head slowly. "Why did you lie to me about her?"

"I...lie?" He furrowed his brow again. "What are you talking about?"

"You acted as if you didn't know that woman and—"

"I don't—"

"Ruben, if you don't want to tell me something, just say so, but don't lie to me. She was talking with you as if you two were friends. I saw you." Blaire tossed aside the shell and pivoted to go back to the house. "Just don't lie. I hate that."

He caught her elbow. "Blaire, okay. I know her from Palm Beach. She's a friend of Earla's."

"So why the lie? What's so terrible about that?"

"Nothing. I just want to start with a clean slate here."

"You can't be clean and still be a liar, Ruben." She knew she'd gone too far by the tightening of the muscles in his jawline. "Look, I should see to those errands so that I'll be back before Molly gets home. You go ahead and enjoy your stroll."

"Could I run those errands for you? It's all part of the job."

"No, thanks. I've got to pick up some art supplies. See you later." She waved at him and jogged away, stung by his artful dodging around the truth. She'd practically had to demand that he be straight with her, and that upset her image of him. He'd seemed so forthright, so open. But there were pockets of mystery in him; forbidden zones he'd lie about to keep trespassers at bay.

Being lied to was a sore spot left over from her marriage. Jimmy had lied to her over and over again about his extramarital activities. The lies hurt almost as badly as the broken promises and ultimate broken heart. Was she attracted to Ruben because some of his characteristics reminded her of Jimmy? That sent a shudder through her, but she examined it, nonetheless. Both were free spirits who had flitted from job to job. Both covered their tracks with half truths and lies. Both were handsome with athletic builds.

Ruben had spoken of wanting to settle down, but Jimmy had said the same thing during their courtship. Tiring of the comparison, Blaire told herself she was putting the cart before the horse. After all, Ruben was her butler and would most likely disappear from her life after two weeks. No use fretting over a man who was just passing through. But the disappointment lingered, making her all the more aware of her own attraction to Ruben. If she cared this much about him after only two days, what would he mean to her after two weeks?

WHEN RUBEN RETURNED from the beach, Blaire was gone. Self-directed anger burned in his gut, and he clenched his teeth to keep from bellowing.

What in bloody hell was with Earla? Couldn't she take a hint? Hint, be damned! He hadn't pussyfooted around with her. He'd told her flat out that it was over between them. What was she thinking, calling up Silent Butler and wrangling Blaire's phone number from them? And now she wanted to visit him in St. Augustine. Too much. It was all too much.

He carried the empty laundry basket into the house. Blaire's perfume hung in the air, and he paused to appreciate it. The anger subsided, and he began to see that he wasn't all that angry at Earla, but at himself for not being truthful with Blaire. Should have told her straight out that he knew Julia Vandermeter, he thought with twenty-twenty hindsight. Now Blaire wouldn't trust him. She'd be wary, overly cautious.

He shrugged off the whole fiasco and told himself he was creating a tempest in a teapot. What if he didn't win her affections? It wouldn't be the end of the world. In fact, now wasn't the ideal time to get personally involved. Not with his restaurant to get shipshape and a business to build.

He set the basket in the utility room and went into Blaire's studio to use the phone there. He'd arrived in St. Augustine a day early and had located a great place for his restaurant. The building had formerly housed a pizza parlor, but he saw immediately it would do nicely for what he had in mind—an intimate bistro with an ever-changing menu. Having contacted the owner, Caymen Lawrence, he had instructed the man to draw up the necessary papers. Ruben punched in Lawrence's business number and asked for him when a secretary answered.

"Caymen Lawrence," a gruff voice said across the line.

"Mr. Lawrence, Ruben Crosscroft here. I was wondering if you have papers for me to sign yet."

"Ah, yes. How you doing, son? Papers . . . let me think. Nope. Guess I need to rattle my attorney's cage, huh? He's supposed to be checking your references."

"I see. Well, do you still have my number here?"

"Yes. My secretary has it. I'll get back to you some time this week. That's a promise."

"Thank you, sir. I'm anxious to move forward on this."

"I understand. I'll be talking to you soon. Don't you worry. I want that place leased just as much as you want to lease it."

"Good. Thanks again." Ruben replaced the receiver and started from the studio, but paused to admire Blaire's work.

Lifting the protective onion-skin sheet, he studied her art. She's good, he thought, admiring the whimsy of her drawings. The expressions on the animals' faces made him think of classic Disney films.

Her drawings of warm, cuddly creatures made him remember his pet name for her—kitten. He hadn't called her that aloud, but the name floated in his mind when he looked at her. He smiled, recalling how flustered she'd been after one kiss. Of course, he didn't have any room to talk. He'd gotten carried away, too. It had been awhile since a woman had managed to shake him up, make him forget himself. He'd always been in control with Earla or her friends, and careful to keep things in their proper perspective. But with Blaire . . . well, she was habit-forming.

After replacing the thin sheet over the drawing, he left her studio behind, but not his thoughts of her. Reflections of her hovered like perfume in still air. Her laugh, her smile, her ups, her downs. God, he sounded like a sixties musical!

Get a grip, mate, he told himself as he filled a bucket with warm water and ammonia, then gathered a huge sponge and old newspapers with which to polish the glass panes. The woman is cute, but don't get so worked up that you'll ruin this sweet deal by coming on strong. She'll kick your butt out the door, and you'll have to spend mucho bucks on a lousy hotel room. He sure didn't want to capsize this dreamboat.

Speaking of troubled waters . . . Earla. He heaved a sigh and hoped to heaven she wouldn't arrive in St. Augustine. He'd made it clear that he was on a job and didn't have a moment to himself. In other words, her trip would be wasted. But he wasn't sure Earla had understood that he was telling her to tear his page out of her book.

She'd never taken him seriously, so she didn't take this stab of respectability and ownership seriously, either. He knew she expected him to eventually drift back to her and the easy life she provided.

His job as chef in Earla's posh restaurant/club had been great, but he'd felt like a koala much of the time, passed from Earla to her condescending friends to be clucked over, stroked and fondled. When Earla had suggested that he take one of her friends to a gallery opening, he'd refused at first. But then Earla had played to his soft heart, telling him that the poor woman's husband was never in town and she didn't feel safe going out alone. She'd pay for his time. He'd agreed to the evening out. That's how it had started. Innocent enough, he thought, remembering how easy it had been to continue as escort to Earla's women friends.

As the money accumulated, he'd realized it might be his ticket out. He'd wanted to have his own place for a while, but never could imagine swinging it, financially. He'd tried getting a bank loan and had been turned down. However, with the money he earned as chef and his moonlighting as escort for Earla's friends, he began to see that he could sock away a nice nest egg. When Earla had offered him the guest house on her property, rent free, he'd accepted since the arrangement would save him even more money.

That's probably when Earla began to see him only as her toy and not as an employee at her restaurant, he thought. More and more, she insisted that he take time off from the restaurant to take her or one of her friends places. Evenings out became long weekends. Weekends became weeks. He went along because his escort fees were triple what he received as Earla's chef. After six months, he'd saved enough money to begin planning his next step. He'd told Earla he'd probably leave her employ by summer, by year's end at the latest.

Earla had tried to entice him to stay put by offering to bankroll his restaurant, but he'd seen through her charity. Her money wouldn't just buy him a business, it would buy him.

"No, thanks," he'd told her. "I want to make my own way. Besides, people might think I'm your loverboy."

"Would that be so bad?" she'd asked.

"For me, yes. Being 'kept' isn't my style."

"Since when?"

The remembered conversation blew through him like a bitter wind, and he felt every muscle in his face tense as he gritted his teeth in outrage. The truth had shamed him. He'd been fooling himself, calling what he did favors to friends. But they weren't his friends. They were his employers. They'd hired him. And not just to escort them. Even now it was hard for him to admit the bald truth. He'd slept with them. Not all of them. Two. But that was enough to make him feel cheap. Sex had been something he'd enjoyed, but it had become work. Work! That still knotted his gut and soured in his heart.

He wondered if he could feel again or if he'd ruined himself for any personal, intimate involvement. Would he be able to make love again without being conscious of his performance, of doing and saying the right thing, of doing a good job? Odds were he would, but he found himself yearning to be swept away, sent into a mindless, passion-filled oblivion. Like an impotent man told he was cured, Ruben ached to test that diagnosis. He wasn't sex-starved. No. Sex, he'd had plenty of. He wanted *to make love* again.

When Earla had sensed his change of heart, she'd tried to placate him by lavishing him with compliments about his culinary skills, but Ruben would have none of it. He'd given his two-week notice and had packed and left on day fifteen.

So why was Earla following him? He wasn't the only blue-collar male in her sandbox. Maybe it was a simple case of pride. Earla wanted to be the one who cut people loose, and it probably galled her that he'd gotten to the scissors first.

Still a little short of his money goal, he'd searched the classifieds for a restaurant job and had seen the ad from the Silver Polish company. They needed a trained butler quick, a position he hadn't held since his early twenties, and then only briefly. The man they'd hired originally had suffered a stroke, leaving them in a pinch. The salary and expense account had enticed Ruben, and he'd charmed the woman who'd interviewed him. He'd been hired and sent to the Blaire Thomlin residence in beautiful St. Augustine.

Ruben stepped outside, bucket and accessories in hand. Grunt work, he thought, picking out the first window to be washed, but he didn't mind. The sun felt great and his ultimate goal loomed ever closer. Even hearing from Earla couldn't dampen his spirits.

He dipped the sponge into the bucket of ammonia water. The fumes soared up and burned his nose. He checked his watch and calculated that he might be able to finish the outside of the windows before Molly or Blaire returned home. Tipping his face to the sun, he basked in the warmth for a few moments before attacking the first sand-speckled window. He worked quickly and had washed six and was heading for the seventh when he heard the front door chimes.

SHIFTING THE SHOPPING bags to one hand, Blaire unlocked the front door and stepped inside. The first thing she noticed was the Brüt, and the smell of it brought a cavalcade of memories—some pleasant, some painful. Then she saw the beat-up, avocado-green Samsonite luggage—one large piece, one shaving kit—and Blaire's heart dropped along with her shopping bags. The matching weekender and makeup case were stored in the attic; they had not been touched since the divorce.

"Hello, Blaire." Jimmy stood up from the sofa and pushed down the wrinkles in the legs of his snug jeans. "Surprised? I bet you didn't think I'd really show up for Molly's party, did you?"

"I thought the odds were against it," she admitted, retrieving her shopping bags. "Have you been here long?" She glanced out the window, spotting the blue sedan parked across the street. A rental, she guessed.

"I've only been here a few minutes. You're looking good, Blaire. Guess life is treating you fair."

He looked pretty good himself, Blaire noted, although his dark hair seemed to be climbing backward and thinning out on top. He still had that great smile, though. Wide and bracketed by dimples. Sometimes that grin could be downright lethal.

Blaire tapped the toe of her sandal against his shaving kit. "Didn't even stop to unpack at your hotel before you came by, I see."

His blue eyes challenged her and his face tensed. Lines radiated from the corners of his mouth; lines that hadn't been there a year ago. Jimmy was thirty, and the blush of youth had faded from his face, replaced by maturity. She wondered if that maturity was only skin deep.

"You've got a guest room, and I'm what you'd call a guest these days, right? I'll get to see a lot more of Molly by staying here. It'll be fun. I won't get in your way."

She set the shopping bags on the coffee table. "Sorry, but someone is using the spare bedroom. Besides, I don't think it's a good idea for you to stay here. I'm busy, and I need my privacy during the day. My home is my office, and I'm on a deadline."

"Who's in the spare bedroom?"

Blaire glanced around, looking for him. "Ruben. He's the butler. He let you in, didn't he?"

"Yes, he did." Jimmy nodded toward the credenza in front of the picture window where a bouquet of daisies had been arranged in a cut-glass vase. "I was expecting you to open the door, so I stuck those out and said something like, 'Guess who, sweet-cheeks.' Talk about embarrassing! Of course, old Prim and Proper didn't even crack a smile."

Blaire hid hers behind one hand. "Where is he?"

"Beats me. I told him I didn't need baby-sitting. What the hell do you have a butler for, anyway?"

Blaire could tell he was miffed, but couldn't fathom why. Did Ruben and Jimmy have words? "Molly won him in a contest. He's only here for two weeks."

"Won him, did she?" Jimmy chuckled and raked a hand through his hair. It all fell back in place, trained by styling gel. "That Molly's the stuff. When does she get home from school?"

Blaire checked her watch. "Any minute now." Movement caught her eye and she swung toward the kitchen. "There you are," she said to Ruben. The front of his shirt was wet; so were his tennis shoes. "What have you been up to?"

"Washing windows."

"Oh, yes. I forgot."

"Can I get anything for you?"

She shook her head and glanced at Jimmy. "Ruben Crosscroft, Jimmy Jacobs," she said, although neither man seemed interested in the introduction. "I was just telling Jimmy—he's Molly's father—about how Molly won you for a fortnight." Why did she feel like a girl caught between two warring boys?

"That's how you make your living?" Jimmy asked, not bothering to look at Ruben, although he was speaking to him. "You rent yourself out? I thought there was a law against that."

Blaire caught Ruben's eye and shook her head, silently telling him to dismiss Jimmy's rudeness. He did so with some difficulty, his bunched hands relaxing ever so reluctantly.

"Guess I could sleep here," Jimmy said, running his hands over the sofa cushions. "I've slept in worse places."

"No, Jimmy." Blaire went to admire the daisies. "Thanks for these, and thanks for coming to visit Molly,

but you're going to have to take that Samsonite somewhere else."

"Why?" Jimmy asked, a defensive edge to his voice.

"Because this is my house," Blaire said, turning to
confront him, and just in time to see Ruben's back as
he disappeared into the kitchen. "And I've got to work
this week. I can't entertain house guests."

"What do you call *him?*" Jimmy asked, jerking a
thumb in the direction of the kitchen. "If you ask me,
it doesn't look good to let a stranger stay here with you
and Mol."

She was about to say, "Nobody asked you," but the
front door swung open and Molly burst inside, spotted Jimmy, then hurled herself into his arms. Watching
the scene, a lump formed in Blaire's throat. Family, she
thought with a wistful sigh. People took family for
granted, but not Blaire. She'd dreamed of being a wife
and a mother, back when she thought the two were in-
separable. Wife and Mother. Can't have one without
the other. Well, she knew better now. Or, rather, she
knew worse.

Looking away from the happy reunion, which had
become painful to watch, Blaire saw Ruben standing in
the kitchen doorway and realized she viewed him
through a film of tears. She blinked and looked away,
embarrassed that Ruben had seen her bout of melan-
choly. A corner of her heart mourned for her lost marriage and family life, but she knew she couldn't have
had that with Jimmy. Maybe she hadn't been the perfect wife, but Jimmy had never even tried to be a faithful husband. She wondered if he'd ever regretted not
trying, not communicating with her, lying through his

teeth when she'd asked him if he was seeing other women. Had the ensuing years shown him the error of his ways?

"Mom, can we?" Molly asked, sitting on Jimmy's lap, her arms secured around his neck.

"Can we what?" Blaire asked, swiping at her eyes to clear them.

"Go out to eat and to the movie. Daddy's treat."

"No, we—" The automatic refusal rang in her ears, and Blaire nixed it. "That is, you two go on."

"Mom, please go with us."

"Come on, Blaire. It'll be like old times. Right, Mol?"

"Right!" Molly giggled under her father's tickling fingers.

Blaire squeezed Molly's short chin affectionately. "Thanks, but I'll use the time to work. You have fun with your daddy." Looking from one to the other, Blaire was struck by the resemblance. Molly's features came from Jimmy, but most of her mannerisms were Blaire's.

"Don't be a wet blanket," Jimmy said, still pitching.

Molly slipped off his lap. "It'll be just you and me, Daddy. I'll change clothes. Be right back." She gave him another smacking kiss on the cheek before racing to her room.

"She's some kind of kid," Jimmy said, looking after Molly, then swinging his gaze meaningfully to Blaire. "We did good."

Blaire smiled wanly. "Yes, at least we salvaged something from the wreckage."

"Oh, it wasn't so bad," Jimmy scoffed. "We had lots of good times."

Blaire laughed, humorlessly. "Maybe you did."

"I've changed, Blaire. Looking back, I can see it was wrong for me to give in to temptation so often. But there were women all over the place. You know how they follow celebrities around."

"Celebrities?" she echoed, amused that he placed himself in that high echelon.

"Well, athletes. People in the spotlight. Women just threw themselves at us. I was on the road and away from you and . . . well, I'm not proud of my behavior back then." He hung his head, right on cue.

Blaire bit back a sarcastic retort. "It's all water under the bridge," she said, proud of herself for not starting a verbal brawl. "Are you seeing anyone? What happened to that woman in Chicago?"

"Chicago?" He blinked, confused, then snapped his fingers. "Oh, right. Her. That's over. There's nobody special in my life right now. I've decided to concentrate on my career."

"Where are you working?"

"I'm not. I'm scouting for just the right offer. The Seattle team might hire me for its promotions department."

Blaire nodded, unsure whether to believe him or not.

"You think that butler could fix me a drink? Scotch and soda will do."

"I don't have any liquor in the house, except for table wine. Besides, you shouldn't drink and drive."

"Oh, right." He rubbed his hands down his jeans legs again in a nervous gesture. "I'm kind of uptight. Seeing you again always gets to me."

Blaire tipped her head to one side, curious. "Why?"

"Because you're so judgmental, and I never meet your standards."

She sighed. "Jimmy, don't feel that way. You don't have to please me anymore." She heard Molly's bedroom door close. "Have fun with your daughter. She loves you so much, Jimmy. You're a giant in her eyes."

"I am?" Jimmy smiled as Molly skipped into his arms and gave him a big hug. He shared a smile with Blaire. "I'll have her back home by eight. Is that okay?"

"That's fine." Blaire led them to the door. Mixed emotions swirled through her. Mostly, she felt angry with herself for not being able to provide her daughter a full-time dad. It had to be hard on Molly.

Blaire grabbed a light sweater off the coat tree. "Ruben, I'm going for a walk," she called, already letting herself out the patio door.

STANDING ON A SAND HILL, Ruben could see Blaire walking slowly along the shoreline, head down, hair blowing across her face, hands clasped behind her back.

The kitten's restless, he thought, letting his gaze drift over her body. She walked into the breeze, and it plastered her pink sweater against her, showing off round, high breasts and a gently concave stomach. Her body could belong to a high school girl instead of to a woman who'd given birth almost nine years ago. She had a flowing gait, graceful and liquid. He termed her as not classically beautiful, but having what fashion photographers called an all-American appeal—blond, tan, green-eyed, and an open, honest face.

He surmised that she'd taken to the beach to mull over her marriage and divorce. He'd known his share of divorced women, and nearly all of them beat themselves up over the failed relationships. He and Jimmy hadn't exactly hit it off, not that he'd tried all that hard to like Jimmy Jacobs or make Jimmy like him. He'd pegged Blaire's ex as a pompous jock who couldn't keep his fly zipped.

He jogged down the hill toward her, his bare feet kicking up white sand. The moist air felt good on his legs and arms, bared by cutoffs and a tank top.

"Hi, there," he said, stopping in front of her. "Sorry to bother you."

"No bother," she murmured, then her expression sharpened as if she'd slipped from the past to the present.

"Getting hungry, I hope?" He grinned, trying to nudge her from her introspective mood. "Your dinner's ready. Broiled steak, mixed veggies, cheese bread. Any of that make your mouth water?"

"All of it." She looked expectantly at him. "Have you eaten yet?"

"No."

"Then will you join me?"

"Be glad to. Thanks." Ruben turned sideways to appreciate the mighty ocean. The sun sat on the horizon, painting the sky orange and pink. "Are you okay, Blaire?" he asked, glancing in her direction. "I mean, is there anything I can do? I'm a good listener."

"Seeing Jimmy always makes me regret so much."

"You mean, you regret the divorce?"

"No. The marriage."

He was surprised by the profound relief that arrowed through him. "Was he an unfaithful husband?"

She whipped her head around, her eyes finding his. "Right on the nose. How'd you know?"

"It's the number one reason for breakups."

She nodded. "That's what broke us up. I was to blame in that I had stars in my eyes and clung to this romantic notion that Jimmy would shape up once he had a wedding ring on his finger."

"You mean, you suspected he was unfaithful before the marriage?"

"Yes." She winced. "Dumb, huh?"

He shrugged, careful not to be too self-righteous. "It's hard for a leopard to change his spots."

"I believed that love was the strongest emotion in the universe and could work wonders. I learned a lot during my marriage. Most of my theories about the power of love were blown to smithereens."

"That's too bad. Love *is* miraculous. You haven't lost your faith in it, have you?"

"No, but I've tempered that faith with human nature." Her gaze skittered from his to the foam stopping inches from her toes. "Oh, look!" Splashing into the surf, she bent to grab at a rolling piece of shell. She caught it and held it aloft, a happy smile curving her lips. "Got it!"

"What?"

"A little conch. They're called something else . . . I forget, but you hardly ever see them washed up around here. Pretty, isn't it?" She held out her hand, palm up, so he could inspect her treasure.

"It's an oyster drill," he said, picking it up between his thumb and forefinger to admire the pale pink interior of the white shell.

"You sound like a man who knows his shells."

"I'm a man who has spent most of his life on islands."

"Oh, that's right. England, Australia. Huge islands." She made an expansive gesture, throwing her arms wide. "I'm used to the smaller varieties. Atolls. Keys."

Ruben thought she looked remarkably young in the favorable light of a setting sun. Her legs were long, slim, firm; her arms, bonelessly graceful; her hands full of an artist's secrets. Does Jacobs look at her and ache with longing? he wondered. Does Jacobs know what he's lost?

Dropping the delicate shell into her palm, he closed her clever fingers around it. "So you don't carry a torch for your ex-husband." He told himself he didn't want to dwell on why this was so important.

"No, that flame was doused long ago. I haven't been thinking about Jimmy. I've been thinking about me. Mother and Molly both agree I'm too defensive, too distrustful. Maybe they're right." She had been staring at the sea treasure, but now her green eyes focused on him. "It's time for me to emerge from my shell and take my lumps—good or bad." She pocketed the oyster drill. "I just wish Molly didn't have to pay for my bad judgment."

"Pay? How do you mean?"

"She has a temporary father because I wasn't wise enough to see that Jimmy would make a lousy husband."

He followed his yearnings and trailed the fingertips of one hand down the side of her face. Up close, he saw a sprinkling of pale freckles across the bridge of her nose and her cheeks. Her lashes were sable-tipped gold. She didn't move away from the caress.

"Molly doesn't seem worse for it. She's a charming child."

"I just wish she had a great father like I do. My dad is always there for me. I don't have to track him down through long distance every time I have a problem."

"She's got you, Blaire, and you're a fabulous mother. You know that, don't you?" When she nodded, her cheek rubbed his hand. He wanted desperately to kiss her, but he felt the timing wasn't right, so he simply draped a casual arm around her shoulders and strolled with her toward the house.

"I've got to get out more. Mother says I'm an Amazon warrior with a kid in tow."

Ruben laughed. "Your mother is wrong. You're no Amazon. You haven't met anyone since your divorce? There's been no man in your life?"

"No. I tried, but I felt so awkward. Dating is tough, you know. I didn't have that much experience at it. I dated a little in high school. I met Jimmy in college, and he was my one and only."

"One and *only*." He eyed her, wondering if she meant that literally or if it was a figure of speech.

They reached the house. Blaire started to open the patio door, but spun around to face him instead. Her eyes seemed enormous in the diffused light. She drew in a shaky breath.

"Yes. One and only. I was a virgin when I married." She laughed nervously. "Old-fashioned, huh? Guess I'm a throwback to a more puritan era. I feel like a damned neophyte. Especially around you."

"Why, especially?"

Color seeped into her cheeks. "You seem to me a man who's known a few women—in the biblical sense."

He grinned. "My share, but I think you're being too hard on yourself." He reached behind her and opened the door.

"I don't know. I think my cautious nature discourages men. It's a turnoff."

"Not true," he objected, finding the conversation incongruous. The woman was talking about turning men off while he tried to tamp down his throbbing libido. He motioned for her to precede him into the house. Her perfume, light and flowery, drifted to him. Passion gnawed at the edges of his patience.

"Not true, huh? Well, you haven't hit on me," she said, then hesitated on the threshold to look over her shoulder at him. "Except that kiss. But that wasn't premeditated. That was an accident."

He saw the glint of mischief in her eyes and realized she was being playful. He moved closer. Her eyes widened and a smile tugged at the corners of her delectable mouth. She stumbled inside, suddenly losing her natural grace. He caught her elbow to steady her.

"You make it sound like murder, Blaire. Second-degree desire instead of first-degree lust." When her gaze drifted to settle on his lips, his heart bumped against his ribs. "And it wasn't an accident. Neither is this."

Ruben pulled her to him, his mouth seeking and finding hers for a sweet, suckling union. No woman should taste so good, he thought, his tongue skimming her satiny lower lip. A whimpering moan rose from her and then her lips separated, bidding him entrance. But he hesitated, in no rush. He cradled her head between his hands, his fingers exploring the thickness of her hair and her nape. She moved more completely against him, one leg sliding between his. Through slitted lids, he saw that her eyes were closed.

"Ruben, Ruben," she whispered against his mouth, then nuzzled the side of his neck. He thought he might die. "I told myself not to let you—that this wasn't right. But here I am and here you are, and I couldn't stop thinking about you and how this would feel...."

He chuckled and sprinkled kisses over her freckled nose, then angled back to drink in the sight of her flushed face. "You have something against cavorting with the hired help?"

"I don't think of you as that," she said, her eyes widening a fraction. "I'm a lot of things, but I'm not a snob."

"Yes." He watched an orangy ray of dying sunlight slant over her face. "You are a lot of things." His heart slammed into his chest wall as he lowered his mouth to hers again.

She brought her hands up to bury her fingers in his hair. Her body felt pliant and delicate in his enfolding embrace. The inside of her mouth was slick and cool, but heated quickly when his tongue stoked the fires. He found the curve of her hips, and his hands splayed wantonly over them. A flash of desire crackled through him, fired his blood and sent his nobility up in smoke. He'd take her. Right here. Right now.

Blaire tore her mouth from his and stepped back. She smoothed her hair from her face with both hands, looking shaken and unsure of her next move. Ruben reached for her, but she retreated.

"No, wait. I . . . this is too fast." She noticed the table set for dinner. "I think I'll change before we eat."

How did women compose themselves so quickly? he wondered. Writhing with passion one moment, making small talk the next. Amazing. Bloody amazing. He looked from her to the table as his thoughts caught up with what she'd said.

"I scared you. I came on too strong."

"No." She shook her head. "It's not you, it's me. I have to go slow, Ruben. Please try to understand."

Reason was returning to his mind, clearing his body of wild passion. "Right. How about a bottle of wine to go with this meal? I've chilled some rosé in the fridge."

"Sounds great." She reached out to trail her fingertips across the back of his hand. "Thanks for understanding."

She turned and went toward her bedroom. Ruben stared after her, wondering what he was supposed to understand. The only thing he comprehended perfectly was the throbbing ache pressing against his fly. He grimaced and ran a hand over his hot face. He forced himself back to the kitchen and back to being the butler.

"TAKE MY MOTHER AND DAD," Blaire was saying, stretched on a chaise longue on the back patio and waving a crystal glass in a sweeping gesture. "They're made for each other. Perfection. They don't realize how lucky they are . . . well, maybe they do." She took a drink of wine. "They are so in love—so into each other—that, growing up, I felt kind of left out at times. But I envy them." She glanced at Ruben, her eyes refusing to focus until she blinked several times. "Does that sound dopey?"

"Not at all." He leaned forward in the deck chair and propped his elbows on his knees. A full moon provided a bright night-light. Though he couldn't see it from where he sat, he knew the ocean would be a bed of black velvet strewn with diamonds. He could hear its gentle roar in the distance. Ruben examined Blaire from the corner of his eyes, trying to tell if she might be a wee bit tipsy. How many times had he refilled her wine glass? One, two, three. He smiled to himself, glad she was no longer tense and awkward as she had been during dinner.

"Do you have any family in the States?" she asked.

He sat back, stretching his arms above his head. "My family is spread out—some in England, some in Australia. I'm the eldest of four and the only boy. Sometimes I miss them."

"What? The footloose loner misses his family?"

"Loners need love, too."

"Sounds like a bumper-sticker slogan," Blaire said, returning his smile, and wondering if he had any idea how drop-dead-gorgeous he looked beneath a full moon. "Ruben Crosscroft, I believe that deep down you're an old softie."

"You've nailed me," he admitted. "I get all mushy over moon-splashed oceans, day-old kittens, tear-jerker movies, certain television ads, especially around Christmas, and the selfless nature of woman."

"You don't think men can be selfless?"

"Mostly selfish, I'm afraid. We have a stronger sense of survival—our own over others. Women tend to fling themselves in the path of certain pain, all in the name of love. Look at your divorces—who usually pays a higher emotional price?"

"Women," Blaire answered automatically.

"Women," Ruben agreed.

"Ruben, are you perchance, a feminist?"

He made a comical face. "A feminist? That goes against my Australian nature, but I will admit my sympathy lies with women. They usually give more to relationships and end up losing more when they're over. They get custody of the children and are expected to provide a stable environment when all hell is breaking loose."

A tightness invaded her chest, and Blaire inhaled a choppy breath that snagged Ruben's attention.

"What's wrong?" he asked, cautiously angling closer to her.

"You..." She started to make something up. I'm chilly. I'm tired. I'm sleepy. I've drunk too much. But honesty won out. "You surprise me. You seem to know women pretty well."

The burden of truth bore down on him, and he wanted to tell her why he knew women so well; that he'd studied them, listened to them, commiserated with them. He took a deep breath and released a tidbit of truth.

"In Palm Beach there are a lot of lonely women, Blaire. Married women, divorced women, widows. The married, lonely ones are the saddest, but the divorced ones can break your heart, too. They were left with lots of money, lots of time and no one to love. Their kids are grown, and they have an empty nest. Their husbands have gone off to find themselves or to be with younger women and begin other families. They're left in the dust—made to feel like dull relics. In a way, you're lucky your marriage ended after a few years and that you had Molly to love and to love you."

Blaire sat forward to see his face better. Sincerity shone in his eyes, and his expressive mouth pulled into a frown. "Were you friends with those women in Palm Beach?"

"Yes." He set his jaw, waiting for her to accuse him.

"You're a sweet, decent man, Ruben Crosscroft."

Ruben's chest caved in under the weight of artificial sainthood. "No, I'm not, Blaire." He stood up, needing to put distance between himself and Blaire's misguided compliment. "I've been meaning to speak to you about Molly's birthday. How many guests do you expect?"

Blaire set down the wineglass. Why had he changed the subject so quickly? "Ruben, did I say something to make you mad?"

"No."

"Then why won't you look at me?"

He turned slowly, his expression taciturn. "How many guests should I prepare for?"

"No more than ten. What did I say to make you adopt your butler routine again? I thought you wanted to be friends. Have you changed your mind about me?"

He shook his head. How could he explain to her that she deserved more than he could possibly give her? She was looking for pure love and for a decent man to be Molly's stepfather. He didn't fit that bill. His recent past prohibited him from the kind of life Blaire offered. Once she discovered what he'd been in Palm Beach, she'd want to wash her hands of him completely. Any association with him would make her feel used, and Ruben already cared too much about her to allow her to feel that way.

"Maybe we should keep this strictly business." It was hard for him to say that, since it wasn't what he wanted.

"Ruben . . ." She stood up and stepped close enough for him to see the sheen of desire in her jewellike eyes. "Are you sure?"

"I . . . oh, hell."

Blaire closed her eyes against a whirlpool of stars and wrapped her arms around his neck. His mouth claimed hers with a ferocious hunger. It had been a long time since she'd wanted a man, heart and soul, but the intensity of that yearning had not diminished with time and infrequency.

She pushed her hands up under his shirt to stroke the tautness of muscle, ribs, furred stomach. He swept the shirt up and over his head and dropped it beside the chaise. Blaire rained kisses across his shoulders and up his throat. His mouth opened under hers, ever the bold hunter. Impatience lashed her, accelerating her pulses and elevating her passion.

"Oh, I want . . . I want you," Blaire whispered between hot, moist kisses. "I feel as if this is right. Tell me it's right, Ruben." She sensed a spear of uncertainty in him. "Ruben, please."

"Blaire . . . Blaire, think about this." He pushed her hands and arms down, away from him.

"I don't want to think. I want to feel." She blinked, trying to focus her eyes, but her vision remained fuzzy. How many glasses of wine had she gulped to erase her nervousness?

"I don't think you really know what you want." He grabbed his shirt, but didn't put it back on. "Do you really want to go to bed with a man you won in a bloody contest?" His glance was sharp and blessedly brief. "A woman like you, a woman who has done quite well for herself—all by herself." He shook his head and gave a derisive laugh. "You could do better than a chef-turned-butler with nothing to show for his life but a handful of dreams." He cleared his throat of quavering emotion. "You could do *a lot* better. Remember what your ex said. I'm rented." Something raw and vulnerable entered his voice. "You don't want someone like me."

"Maybe it's you who doesn't want someone like me."

"Blaire, you know better than that." He sighed and raked both hands through his hair. His eyes burned as he looked at her and knew he couldn't hide from her anymore. "Back in Palm Beach . . ."

"What? What is it, Ruben?" She touched him, but drew away when his gaze sliced through her. "Tell me."

Contrition twisted his mouth. "Back in Palm Beach I moonlighted as an escort."

"An escort?" She shook her head, confused.

"You heard right."

She laughed, her thoughts refusing to solidify. "So, you took women out on dates and they paid you?" She flinched at the hard glare he delivered. There was a challenge in it, and the import sobered her for a few startling moments. A vile word dropped into her mind. "A gigolo?" Her voice came out husky, gruff.

"Some would have called me that, I guess. I didn't do it for long. Just a few months to get enough money to finance my restaurant." He frowned at her. "Why are you backing up? I was an escort, not a rapist."

Blaire made herself stand her ground. "I can't believe this. You—you should have told me this before now."

"I know. Guess I'm not such a sweet, decent man, huh?"

She swallowed and the stars spun around her. "I don't know. I can't think clearly. I should go to bed." She pressed a hand to her forehead where a headache was taking hold. Too much wine. If he'd just seduced her, she could handle it, but this true-confession routine was too complicated for a woman who'd drunk more than she had in years. "Let's talk about this tomorrow when I'm not so . . . so . . ." She hiccuped. "Sloshed," she finished, already turning away from him and moving unsteadily inside the house and to her room.

Ruben tossed aside his shirt and tipped back his head to stare at the immensity of sky. Regrets rained down on him, and he wished he could turn back time. Too late for that, he knew. He not only felt helpless, he felt worthless. And there was no one around to blame but himself.

7

AFTER GETTING MOLLY off to school, Blaire went to her studio and closed the door, but she wasn't surprised to hear Ruben's soft knock minutes later.

"Come in." Blaire swiveled on the high stool to face Ruben. "I suppose you want to talk about last night?"

He shut the door and leaned against it. "Now that you've slept on it, what's your verdict?"

"You should have told me before you moved into my house."

He crossed his arms against his chest. "Blaire, I'm prize winnings. A few days ago I didn't think you deserved or would be interested in the story of my life."

"Not your life, just one important aspect of it." She flung a finger in the general direction of Molly's bedroom. "I have an impressionable eight-year-old to protect!"

He narrowed his blue eyes. "If you think for one second that I'd harm a hair on that child's head, then I'll pack up this minute and clear out." He thrust his chin forward. "You think I'm a pervert now?"

"Of course, I don't think that." She dropped her head forward, stretching the kinked muscles in her neck and shoulders. "I drank too much last night. I shouldn't have let you . . . what I'm trying to say is that I've only known you for a few days and I have no right to judge you."

"Your opinion matters to me. Blaire, I'm not unfeeling or insensitive. I don't use women. I think people are together for all sorts of reasons and love is only one of them."

"And your reason was money?" She made herself look at him and immediately wished she'd kept her mouth shut. Color drained from his face and a muscle ticked just below his left ear.

"It was for a brief period. It all started innocently. Do you want me to leave, Blaire?"

She stared at her tightly clasped hands. "No." She was torn between asking about his past and sweeping it under the rug. After several seconds, she decided to put her avid curiosity on hold. She didn't *really* want to know the details . . . did she? "What you suggested last night—strictly business—I think that's a good idea. I've still got a deadline, a birthday party and an ex-husband to juggle. I'd appreciate your help. Also, Molly would be crushed if you up and left. She'd blame me."

"So you want me to stay."

"Yes, as the butler." She caught his tight, tense nod. "The party's Saturday at noon. Here are the invitations." She handed him the envelopes she'd addressed last night when she hadn't been able to sleep. "Please mail them. I'm expecting about a dozen guests. No more than fifteen. Whatever you need, let me know."

"Do you have a preferred menu?"

"No, whatever you think kids will like is fine."

"I have an appointment Friday with the man I'm going to lease from. It's at ten, but I'll be back by noon. Is that okay?"

"Yes."

"Blaire, I'm sorry about this. I wasn't going to tell you, but you insisted on the truth. You said honesty is important to you. I was trying to do the right thing for you."

"Honesty is best. Sometimes it hurts like the dickens, but it's better than lies." She released a quick sigh. "Look, we'll make the best of it. There's a strong attraction between us." She glanced sharply at him. "Isn't there, or am I off base?"

"There is, and it's powerful."

She nodded, oddly relieved. "Which makes this awkward. Anyway, it's probably best if we avoid personal subjects."

He opened his mouth to say something, but shut it.

"What is it?"

"Nothing." He turned and opened the door. "It's all been said. If you need anything, give a shout."

"Ruben." Blaire picked up an artist's brush and examined its sable tip, unable to look directly at Ruben. "Thanks for telling me before I—that is, before we became intimate."

"Guess that won't happen now."

Her gaze lifted unerringly to his, and her heart pulsed with lost chances. She didn't have to reach very deep to recall his hot, honeyed kisses or the warm, satiny feel of his skin. No man had ever aroused her so completely, so quickly, and the wine was only partly to blame. She'd wanted him, and if he hadn't pushed her away and told her about his past, she would have surrendered willingly to his expert hands and lips and tongue.

The doorbell chimed, shattering the silence that shimmered with regrets and sweet memories.

"I'll get it," Ruben said, and closed the studio door.

Blaire slumped over her worktable. She heard her mother's voice. A minute later Agatha tapped on the door and came in.

"Working hard or hardly working?"

"Hardly working." Blaire motioned to the director's chair. "Have a seat. Where have you been, all dolled up?"

Agatha glanced at her smart black silk jumpsuit. "I went to a historical society meeting. We're planning a Ponce de León Day this summer during the height of tourist season. It's a joint effort between St. Augustine and Jacksonville." Agatha studied the sketches on the wall; works in progress. "Are those rejects or just ideas?"

"Early rejects. Actually, I've only this one sketch to finish and I can ship off my Donner Rabbit illustrations."

"Wonderful! Let me see." Agatha stood behind Blaire and admired each charcoal drawing. "Nice work. It's no wonder you're in such demand. You're one talented lady, darling." She kissed the top of Blaire's head, then returned to the canvas chair. "What do you have on tap after this?"

"I signed a contract to do a series of wood-nymph Christmas cards for Touchstone Greetings."

"I thought you weren't interested in that project."

"I wasn't until they offered me enough money to pay off my mortgage. That got me *real* interested."

"Money sweet-talks," Agatha agreed. "What's been happening around here? Anything fun?"

Blaire thought she might burst out laughing, but the urge passed quickly. "Jimmy showed up yesterday."

"No kidding. I really thought he'd be a no-show."

"Me, too. He took Molly out to eat and see a movie last night. They had a grand time, according to Molly. He's been a perfect gentleman around me."

"Blaire, he's not looking good to you again, is he?"

"Heavens, no!" Blaire shuddered. "Give me credit for a little intelligence, Mother."

"Then what's wrong?"

"Why do you think anything's wrong?"

"You have dark circles under your eyes. Are you working night and day on this *Donner Rabbit* project?"

"No."

"Then what? Tell your mother before I nag it out of you."

"It's Ruben."

"Did he hit on you?"

Blaire nodded. "But that's not the problem."

"Right. Who said that would be a problem? He's gorgeous."

"It's about his past, Mother."

"Uh-oh." Agatha bit her lower lip and stood up, pacing to the window. "Has his past caught up with him already?"

"What do you mean, already?" Blaire narrowed her eyes as her thoughts sharpened. "Mother, do you know about what Ruben used to do in Palm Beach?"

Agatha turned to offer a sheepish smile. "When your father checked on him, he uncovered some ugly innuendos."

"And you didn't tell me about them?"

Agatha spread out her hands. "Darling, it was all rumors."

"Mother, you kept this information from me? You let me open my home to a gigolo?"

Agatha widened her green eyes. "Ooo, a gigolo! He admitted to that, did he? I just thought he was involved with a very generous woman. Was it more than one?"

"I don't know. I suppose so."

"Didn't he tell you?"

"I didn't ask and I didn't want to know. That he made a living that way is enough!" Blaire sank her chin in her hand and stared blindly at the drawing on her worktable.

"Darling, he didn't make his living like that. I know for a fact that he was a chef at a fashionable restaurant in Palm Beach."

"And he slept with the woman who owns it," Blaire said. "I don't know for sure, but I think he worked for her in other endeavors, too. She called here looking for him."

"You think he's still with her?"

"Mother, I don't know." Blaire slid off the stool and went to stand beside Agatha at the window. "I was beginning to think he was Mr. Right. He seemed so decent."

"Blaire, if you don't know why he did what he did, you shouldn't condemn him."

"I'm not condemning him, but I have to be careful. It's not just me I have to think of, Mother. The next time around I want to be sure I provide a good man to be Molly's stepfather."

"Keep an open mind, Blaire."

"I'm beginning to wonder if I should trust my judgment where men are concerned."

"Oh, don't be so melodramatic." Agatha placed an arm around Blaire's waist. "And don't throw the baby out with the bathwater."

"I'm not throwing him out, but I told him we should keep our relationship impersonal."

"Well, that's your decision, dear. You might not think he's so terrible if you hear him out. After all, he wasn't *sneaking* around, was he? The women knew exactly what was going down, as your father would say. They hired him. I don't think he solicited, do you?"

"No, I don't think so."

"Maybe he only escorted them. Maybe sex never entered into it."

"Maybe, but I doubt it. I hope he was discreet and . . . careful."

"He's never been in any trouble with the law, Blaire. Your father is convinced he's harmless. He simply fell into an unfortunate life-style in Palm Beach." Agatha turned her around to face her and fluffed the hair curling around Blaire's face. "So, is the party set for Saturday?"

"Yes, at noon. You and Daddy can come?"

"Of course. Wouldn't miss it." Agatha glanced at the wall clock. "I have to dash off. Will you be okay with this?"

Blaire nodded and hugged her mother. "Thanks for dropping by right when I needed you. You've always had impeccable timing."

Agatha kissed her, then rubbed off the lipstick she'd smeared on Blaire's cheek. "Now, remember, Blaire. We all do dumb things from time to time, darling. Even you're not immune." Agatha's green eyes flashed with humor. "After all, you married Jimmy Jacobs."

Laughing, Blaire walked arm in arm with her mother to the front door. "Tell Daddy hello for me. I'll see you both Saturday." As she was closing the front door, the phone started ringing. "I'll get it," Blaire called to Ruben, then plucked the receiver from its cradle. "Hello?"

"Hi, Blaire."

"Oh, hello, Jimmy." She sank onto the couch.

"I have a great idea."

"What?"

"Let me take you and Molly out to dinner tonight."

"Jimmy, that's nice of you. . . ." Blaire's voice faded as her choices became clear. Being with Jimmy and Molly suddenly seemed better than a tense evening spent with Ruben. During the day they were both busy with their work, but she knew that by nightfall they'd have to bump into each other. She also knew she was a chicken for running away from Ruben's company, but she opted for the easy way out, anyway. "What time?"

"You'll go?" Jimmy sounded flabbergasted.

"Sure. Thanks for asking. What time?"

"Six?"

"We'll be ready."

"Great! Well, see you later then."

"Later. 'Bye, Jimmy." She replaced the receiver, resigned to the lesser of two ordeals.

THE DAYS AND NIGHTS that crept toward Saturday seemed the longest in Blaire's life. Her dinner out with Jimmy and Molly had been the beginning of consecutive evenings out. Blaire fretted that Jimmy and Molly might get the wrong idea about her joining them. She even took Molly aside and explained to her that it didn't mean her dad and mom were getting back together.

She was simply escaping from the butler's temptation, Blaire thought while taking her shower Saturday morning. Molly was already up and dressed, skipping through the house in happy anticipation of her birthday party. Blaire took her time showering and toweling herself off, then generously dusted her body with perfumed powder. Selecting an off-the-shoulder sundress of white eyelet, she examined herself critically in the bathroom mirror. She gave her blond, shoulder-length hair fifty strokes of the brush and applied her makeup carefully. All the while her thoughts kept flitting to Ruben Crosscroft.

"The man has bewitched me," she murmured.

Since Ruben had confessed his dubious past, Blaire had struggled with an insatiable curiosity. Her discussion earlier that week with her mother about Ruben had fueled it. Each night, after Jimmy had retired to his motel room and Molly was safely tucked in, Blaire had lain awake, her mind filled with images and scenarios. She'd wondered what sort of women had hired Ruben as an escort. Married women? He'd mentioned them, but mostly he'd talked about divorced women—just like Blaire. Were divorcées his specialty? Did he have a specialty? How many had he bedded in the line of duty?

Carnal notions buzzed through her, made her pulse thrum, sent fantasies of Ruben's legendary lovemaking to plague her. He must be good, she'd reasoned, if women willingly *paid* him. To a woman whose husband had been a midget in the Casanova department, this was heady stuff; the stuff of dreams so erotic that Blaire had awakened several times drenched in sweat, breathless and achy.

Blaire wrenched open the bathroom door and charged into the bedroom. She stumbled to a halt when her gaze collided with Ruben's. He'd been in the process of making her bed. He held one of her pillows, and Blaire couldn't tell if he'd been fluffing it or smelling it. From the tint of pink coloring his ears, she surmised he'd been sniffing the remnants of her perfumed shampoo.

"I . . . uh . . ." She clamped her teeth together for a second to halt her stuttering. "Big day today." *How lame*, she thought, almost groaning aloud, undone to have discovered him in a moment of weakness.

"Yes, it is." He tugged a satin sham over the pillow and positioned it against the headboard. "Everything's ready for the party."

Blaire sat in the upholstered chair to slip on her white pumps. Besides his proper dark suit, white shirt and tie, Ruben wore a faint scowl, and it occurred to Blaire that he'd been in a gray mood ever since he'd returned Friday from his business meeting.

"Ruben, did your meeting go well?"

"What?"

"Yesterday. You met with someone about leasing a building?"

"Caymen Lawrence is the landlord. It didn't go as well as I'd hoped."

"Why not?"

"Oh, I got stabbed in the back." He shoved the drapes away from the windows with more force than was necessary.

"I don't want to pry, but who stabbed you? The landlord?"

"No, one of the people I listed as a reference."

Blaire lounged in the chair, leaping to conclusions. "Earla knifed you, did she?"

His gaze whipped to her. "How'd you know?"

Blaire shrugged. "Intuition. A woman scorned, and all that. She did a number on you?"

"Sort of. When asked to vouch for me, she declined. It wasn't what she said, but what she didn't say. Mr. Lawrence's attorney ran a background check because of Earla's reluctance to endorse me, and it was decided I was a poor risk. No deal."

"No deal?" She shared his disappointment. "Oh, Ruben, I'm sorry."

He stuck his hands in his trouser pockets and stared gloomily out the bedroom window. "I know how those nude models feel now."

"What models?"

"You know, those young women who pose nude for magazines, and then are crucified for it later. The pageant winners, the actresses. They reach for the brass ring and get it snatched from their grasp because of a moment's bad judgment. Their lucky breaks break their backs."

"Ruben, I'll give you a reference if it'll help."

His gaze slid to her like oiled silk. "You'd lie for me?"

"Lie? No. I wouldn't have to lie."

He smiled, but his eyes held no warmth and his tone chilled her. "But you don't think I'm fit company. How could you endorse me with a clear conscience? A man you can't stand being near?"

"Ruben, you're being silly." She stood and started for the door, but was brought up short by Ruben's firm grasp on her upper arm. "Let go."

"In a minute. I just want you to know something, Blaire Thomlin." His gaze flickered over her tanned shoulders and the gentle swell of her breasts above the low neckline. "I'm not dirt. I'm not scum. The women I befriended were consenting adults."

"I've never paid a friend for his or her company."

"Well, that's because you're perfect. You're a blooming saint, you are! Instead of giving me phony references, a couple of my friends invested in my future. They wanted to help me reach my goal. That, to my mind, is the best kind of friend to have."

Stung by his twist on her generosity, she wrenched her arm from his grasp. "I was offering to help you, not insult you, Ruben."

"You were throwing crumbs to a rat," he said with a sneer.

"Look, what you do is your business. You don't have to please me or get my approval."

"Damn straight." He glared at her beneath lowered brows. "That's why it irritates the hell out of me that I should care what you think. I shouldn't give a jot, but I do. That you'd prefer the company of a man who humiliated you to mine cuts like a knife, Blaire." He thrust his face close to hers and repeated through clenched teeth, "Like a knife." Then he opened the bedroom door and strode toward the kitchen, his sacred domain.

Blaire stormed after him, intent on giving him a piece of her mind. His preaching to her about spending time with her ex-husband infuriated her. She burst into the kitchen, but her anger was vanquished by the sight of a three-tiered birthday cake sitting in the center of the table. Molly sat before it, chin propped in her palms, eyes wide with delight.

"Mom, look at my cake! Isn't it the most beautiful one you've ever seen? Ruben made it special just for me."

"It's remarkable," Blaire admitted, coming closer to examine the confectioner's dream. Swathed in pale pink icing, it was topped with pastel-pink-and-wine-colored roses. Thin vines and glossy leaves wound around and around it, all spun from sugary icing. Vines circled candles atop the cake and also formed the salutation Happy Birthday, Molly M'Love. Blaire smiled. With tears burning her eyes and her heart swelled with gratitude, she lifted her gaze to Ruben. "Thank you. You've created something special for my daughter, something she and I will always remember."

He cleared his throat. "Glad to do it."

Dizzying attraction spiraled through her, and she focused her attention on the cake again instead of his darkly lashed eyes.

"Mom, after my party can I go to Cathy's house for an overnight? Her mom says it's okay and can be part of my present from Cathy. Please, Mom?"

Blaire straightened the collar on Molly's blouse. "I guess that will be okay. You haven't planned something with your dad?"

"No. You think he'll mind?"

"I don't think so. I'm sure he'll understand."

The doorbell chimed and Molly squealed and raced to answer it. "They're here! My party's starting!"

Blaire laughed at her daughter's exuberance, but sobered when she looked at Ruben again. "Ruben, we should talk after the party," she said, needing to clear the air between them, once and for all.

He shrugged. "Fine. We'll talk."

Blaire ran a fingertip along the edge of the cake plate, scooping up icing, then popped the delicious treat into her mouth. She closed her eyes for a moment of pleasure. "Eat your heart out, Julia Child," she quipped, then went to welcome the first guests.

Ruben stared after her, playing over and over again in his mind those moments when she'd sucked icing off her finger. Every little thing the woman did aroused him. The past three days had been hell and the evenings had been worse. He'd watched Jimmy Jacobs collect Blaire, take her to dinner and God only knew what else, while Ruben pressed his face against the window and pined like a poor kid wishing for an expensive toy. Even news of Earla's vindictive slap in the face hadn't stung as much as knowing that Blaire couldn't bear to be around him anymore.

So, she wanted to talk. Well, so did he. Molly would be away for the evening, as would Jimmy. It would be him and Blaire, and he'd tell her he was moving out. He'd had enough. He'd honor his second week, but not as her live-in butler. Since Earla had sabotaged his plan to lease Lawrence's building, he didn't have to save every cent. He was more concerned with saving what was left of his pride.

8

RUBEN FINISHED LOADING the dishwasher, smiling at the
memory of Molly blowing out the candles on her
birthday cake and then air-mailing him a kiss. Her
young friends had been impressed. Dex had taken nu-
merous pictures of the sweet creation. Ruben figured
that Dex and Agatha had snapped at least two rolls of
film before taking their leave.

When he thought of Molly's shining eyes and air-
carried kiss, tenderness ballooned in him. A sweet
child, he thought. Enchanting, precocious, flinging her
love hither and yon as if she had more than enough for
the whole world. Maybe she did.

Listening, Ruben realized all was quiet on the birthday front. Had Molly left already to spend the night
with Cathy? He knew Jimmy had bid them good-day
after receiving a phone call and mumbling something
about having an urgent appointment. Straightening
from the dishwasher, Ruben turned to find Blaire
standing just inside the kitchen.

"Need something?"

She shook her head. "Everybody's gone. It was a
great party, Ruben. Thanks."

He shrugged off her gratitude. "All part of the job."
He gritted his teeth, afraid he might say something else
equally inane. *Why did she have to wear that dress?* he

wondered miserably. How was a man expected to cut loose from a woman wearing a tantalizing bit of white lace that left golden shoulders, slim arms and shapely legs bare? "Want a cup of coffee? I've brewed some."

"That sounds great." She eased into one of the kitchen chairs. "Jimmy left early. Did you notice?"

"Yes. Did it have something to do with the phone call?"

"I think so." She looked up from her study of her shell-pink fingernails. "Was it a man or woman calling him?"

Ruben resisted the need to ask her if she really cared. "Woman." He watched her reaction as he placed the cup of coffee before her. A frown tugged at the corners of her mouth. "Does that upset you?"

"What?"

"That a woman called for him?"

"No. I just hope he's not in some kind of trouble. He tends to step into one pile after another."

Ruben chuckled at her analogy and sat opposite her, cradling his cup between his hands. "Well, he's a grown man and you shouldn't worry about him."

She chuckled this time. "I stopped worrying about Jimmy years ago." She lifted her gaze slowly, knowing even before her gaze met his that he was staring at her with jarring intensity. She was acutely aware of him and seemed to take her breaths in sync with his. Blaire couldn't recall having felt such a fascination about a man. Was it because she'd forbidden herself his attentions? Now that she couldn't have him, did that make her want him all the more? She sipped her coffee, never taking her gaze from the beauty of his blue eyes.

"I've come to a decision, Blaire."

She didn't like the tone of his voice. "Oh? About what?"

"I've decided to move out."

Blaire set her cup down with a thump. "But we're supposed to have you for another whole week!"

"And you will. I'll come by every morning and report to work. I'll stay until after dinner and then go to a motel . . . or hotel. I'll book a room somewhere near here."

"Oh, that's silly."

"No, silly is you leaving your house every night so that you won't stumble into me. Now *that's* silly."

"Ruben . . ." She sighed. "Molly will be upset if you move out before your time is up."

"She'll get over it."

"You're doing this just because I joined Molly and her father for dinner a few evenings? Am I not allowed a social life while you're in residence?"

"A social life? You call going out with your ex-husband a social life? Lady, you *are* deprived."

Irritated, Blaire shifted and thought about making a huffy exit, but remembered her promise to talk with Ruben rationally, fairly. "Mother and Dad heard about your extracurricular activities in Palm Beach before I did."

His cocky grin slipped. "They know people in Palm Beach?"

"Dad did a background check on you." She caught the flash of anger in his eyes and rushed to explain. "I couldn't let you move in here with me and Molly without knowing something about you, Ruben. You could have been a child molester or a con man. I couldn't just assume that Silent Butler company would have checked you out thoroughly."

"So your father used his police contacts to see if I had a record?"

"That's right. When Mother came over here earlier this week, I told her about what you'd said and she admitted that Dad had heard some rumors about you being a kept man."

"I wasn't a kept man," he bit out, rising from the chair to dump the remains of his coffee down the sink. "You know what your problem is? You jump to conclusions. I tell you something when you're three sheets to the wind and you fill in the blanks." He turned and leaned back against the sink, arms and ankles crossed, a chilly smirk on his face. "You'd make a lousy judge. You'd dole out life sentences without ever cross-examining the accused."

"Look, you're the one who told me you're a gigolo—"

"You supplied that word, not me."

"Okay, an escort. Same thing. Women hired you for . . . for . . ."

"To escort them to public functions," he finished for her. "Get your mind out of the gutter, luvvy." He enjoyed the flags of color rising in her cheeks.

"Nothing intimate?" she charged. "That's what you're telling me? You never slept with any of those women."

"You make it sound as if I serviced a stableful!" He laughed. "I can count them on one hand."

"Please, do."

He saw that she was serious, so he lifted one hand and extended his index finger, then the middle one, his ring finger . . . his pinkie. "There," he said to her uplifted brow. "I bet Jimmy the Jock bedded more women than that."

Blaire scowled at his nickname. "Probably, but they didn't pay him."

"Oh, no?" He cocked his left eyebrow. "Are you sure about that? Maybe I'm just more honest about it than Jimmy."

She didn't argue, since he, no doubt, was right. Jimmy hadn't charged a fee for his company, but she knew women had paid his rent at times and his phone bills, his dinner bills, bought him clothes.

"I didn't sleep with all of them. Just one or two."

"Which? One or two?"

He shrugged. "Three."

"Three out of four. That's not bad," she said sarcastically. Why was she jealous? After all, if she wanted him she could still have him. Did she still want him? Was that why she cringed when he mentioned the other women in his life?

"I know you think this is a sordid business, but it wasn't like that for me . . . at first."

"At first?"

"At first I was doing favors for some friends. There were a couple of women who came in two or three times a week for lunch at the restaurant where I worked."

"The one Earla owns?"

"Yes. They're friends of hers. She introduced me to them, and we all got on well. Earla asked me to take one of them—her name is Beverly—to an art gallery opening. It was a black-tie affair, and Bev didn't want to go stag. It seemed innocent enough to me. Bev's a widow and lonely. The last man she dated lifted two Cartier necklaces and a Winslow Homer original before he disappeared. Naturally, her trust had been shaken, but she trusted me. So I escorted her to the opening and she insisted on paying me for my time. That was Earla's idea, actually, but Bev thought it was only fair. She said she'd rather pay up front than have somebody take something from her behind her back. The setup gave her piece of mind—and I needed the money."

"Why didn't you just go to your bank and get a loan?"

"Because I have no credit history or collateral, and the banks and savings-and-loans institutions have seen better days. They aren't loaning money to anyone questionable. Believe me, I checked out every bank in and around Palm Beach and they all turned me down." He filled his coffee cup again. "Earla said she believed in me and that this arrangement was the same as back when wealthy people acted as benefactors or patrons to artists, architects and other creative sorts. I wanted to open my own place and Earla and a couple of her friends offered to help—not by *giving* me money, mind you, but by paying for my time."

"Your time and . . . other things." Her gaze drifted down his body of its own free will.

"Mostly my time. These women get invited to all kinds of things, and it's unacceptable for them to show up without an escort. Taking them to parties and openings and benefits wasn't my idea of entertainment. It was work and I was paid by the hour."

"Was sleeping with them a job, too? Did you get time-and-a-half for that?"

He scowled at her. "Tacky," he said, so softly she barely heard him. He took a quick, sharp breath. "Okay, if I talk to you about this, will you listen with an open mind and lose the sarcasm?" He confronted her boldly. "After all, I don't have to tell you a bloody thing, do I?"

She curled her legs up against her and wrapped her arms around them. Avid curiosity wiped out her puritan streak. She was glad of that. What a life this man had led! In comparison, she felt like a convent-raised schoolgirl. She wasn't about to pass up the chance to hear firsthand about his amorous adventures. It was like having the Donahue show in her own kitchen.

"Go on. My mind is wide open."

"Good." He took a gulp of coffee. "The sex thing just sort of happened. After going out several times with Bev, I felt close to her. One night, I returned her to her place late and it was raining buckets outside. She suggested I stay until it let up. She opened some champagne and started telling me how lonely she'd been since her husband had died. I felt sorry for her and I understood her loneliness. One thing led to another . . . well, I spent the night." His glance was shy; however, scorn edged his voice. "She didn't pay me extra and I didn't ask." He took another drink of coffee and released a long sigh. "But she told Carol, a friend of hers, and another woman I'd escorted. Carol Davis was the first one to offer to pay me for a whole evening."

Blaire stopped herself from asking pointed questions that would make her sound like a voyeur.

"I know what you're thinking," Ruben said. "And I did feel funny about the whole thing at first, but Carol had her reasons for asking. She'd had some major surgery that had left scarring, and she was afraid to be intimate with anyone . . . she was afraid some callous oaf would make an unkind remark about her body." He ran a hand down his face, and his voice came out huskier than usual. "I like to think I helped her regain her self-confidence."

When he didn't continue, Blaire cleared her throat to get his attention. "That's two. Beverly and Carol. Who are the other two?"

"I escorted one other lady—strictly as an escort. Merrylu Roffleson. Then there's Earla Nivens."

"She's number three?"

"Yes, and she made me see that my second job had gotten out of hand."

"How did she do that?"

"She got jealous of the other women and decided she wanted me all to herself. I worked for her during the day, and I lived in a guest house on her property. One day I came home from work to find that she'd moved me into the main house with her. Cheeky, huh?"

"Did you object?"

"Sure I did, but Earla said she was having the guest room remodeled and had moved me into the main house so I wouldn't be inconvenienced. Of course, I'm not stupid. I knew she'd staked her claim. Bev told me later that Earla had called her and Carol and Merrylu and told them I was no longer in the escort business. I didn't do anything about it for a couple of weeks." He drew a deep breath. "But when she hired another chef to free my time for her, that was the last straw. We argued. She cried. We said terrible things to each other. She issued an ultimatum that amounted to shape up or ship out."

"You booked passage."

He laughed. "That's right, but not before I lined up the job with Silent Butler."

"What about that woman in the grocery store?"

"That woman...?" He nodded. "Oh, yes. Julia Vandermeter. She's a friend of Earla's, and I never escorted her or anything." He set his cup aside. "Do you still think I'm filth?"

"I never thought that about you," she said earnestly. "I'm just...it's hard for me to imagine anyone paying for a date, that's all."

"Wealthy women attract all kinds of leeches, Blaire. They're used to paying for quality, and I'm top of the line, kitten. Top of the line."

He grinned mischievously, his eyes sparkling, and she had to laugh with him. Her feeble resolve to ward off her attraction to him crumbled and left her with a deep, disturbing yearning. Visions of him making love to grateful women swam through her mind, tormenting her, tantalizing her. Hearing him out hadn't stemmed her tide of longing for him. If anything, it had heightened it. A few seconds later, she registered his nickname for her. "Kitten? You called me kitten?"

He ducked his head, momentarily uneasy. "Yes, well, it suits you." He stood up: straight, tall, broadshouldered. "Speaking of packing, that's what I should be doing. Thanks for hearing me out, Blaire. I didn't want to leave without having you hear my explanation. I understand that you might think my moonlighting job was despicable, but I never saw it like that. Only in hindsight did I see how my escort sideline might ruin any future relationships—especially when I met you."

"What do I have to do with it?" She could barely force the words out.

"You're a good woman and I'm attracted to you." He sighed, concentrating on how to put his feelings into words. "I knew in my gut that you'd think my dealings with Earla and her friends were sordid, and I dreaded telling you. But then you gave your speech about honesty and I knew I'd have to spill the beans, as you Yanks say."

"And I reacted on cue, didn't I?"

"Well, it wasn't as bad as I'd imagined. I thought you might haul off and slap my face, then order me out of your house. Actually, that might have hurt less than having you avoid me the last few days. That's why I'm leaving, Blaire. I can't stand it anymore."

Ruben would have left the kitchen, but Blaire caught his hand and held on. She stared up into his face, silently asking him not to walk out.

Looking down at her, Ruben's hopeful heart soared. Her eyes seemed uncommonly large and her hair shimmered like spun gold. The skin below his stomach tingled and tightened. He had never wanted a woman more in his life.

"Don't go, Ruben. I don't want to be the reason for you leaving before it's time."

"It *is* time, Blaire. I know I make you uncomfortable and I—"

She shook her head. Yes, yes, he made her uncomfortable, but not for the reasons he'd cited. The sexual tension crackling between them made her wonderfully uncomfortable. She squirmed and gripped his hand in both of hers.

"Now that we've talked . . . it'll be different between us. Tell me something?"

"What?"

"Do you miss that life? Do you miss Earla and those other women?"

"No."

"Not at all?"

"Not at all."

Blaire took her courage in hand. "And when you leave my house, will you miss me?"

Every pulse in his body came to life, and he felt an ache so keen that he growled. He cupped her face in his hands, and she rose up from the chair to meet his mouth.

"Miss you? Will I miss you?" he repeated, his lips rubbing hers. "What do you think?"

She couldn't think. Not with his lips stroking hers. Not with his thumbs massaging her throbbing temples. Not with his thigh pressed intimately between hers. She covered his hands with her own and raised up on tiptoes to exchange quick, sipping kisses.

"I think you should stick it out," she whispered. "Molly will—"

"Let's leave Molly out of this. This is between you and me. Strictly grown-up stuff."

Then he showed her exactly what he meant. His lips parted over hers, and the tip of his tongue skimmed her teeth before darting inside. He caught her hands and brought them around him. His arms embraced her, molding her to his length. His masculine essence permeated her every pore as his body kissed hers in an unbroken line from chest to knees. His mouth drifted to her ear, and his teeth nipped at the pearl stud in her lobe.

"Blaire, you're a confusing woman, a luscious puzzle, a riddle of the most fetching kind."

"Mmmm, keep talking. I love to hear you. Your accent is so sexy." She rubbed her cheek against his, thrilling at the scrape of bristle. His after-shave teased her nostrils. She kissed him beneath his jawline and nuzzled him, gathering in the spicy scent.

"I take it that you want me to stay here."

"Clever man."

"You want me to stay here and spend eight more nights in bed alone, aching for you, barely able to stay in my room for want of you. You must think I'm a man of steel, luv. Sorry, but I'm not."

"Not a wooden, sexless butler. I know. I remember."

He gripped her shoulders and held her at arm's length. "I'm not getting through to you, am I?"

"Yes, I hear you. Kiss me again, Ruben. Touch me . . . here." She guided his hand from her shoulder to her breast.

"Blaire, listen to me." He squeezed the pliant flesh, then tugged his hand out from beneath hers. "I like to cuddle and pet and neck, but my libido demands more than that. You haven't had a man in a while—"

"It hasn't been *that* long," she objected, and he gave her a chiding glare from under the shelf of his lowered brows. "What's that got to do with this, anyway?"

"Everything. I can't stay here with you and be satisfied with soul kisses, smoldering looks and the smell of your perfume on the linens and in the bathroom and every other damn place." He ran a hand through his hair in obvious frustration, and Blaire chewed on her lower lip to keep from grinning at his misery. "I've got to have you, Blaire. If I stay, that is."

She nodded, certain of what she wanted, of who she wanted. "So, what are you waiting for, an engraved invitation?"

He blinked, clearly confounded, then desire grew steadily in his blue eyes. "Blaire, I . . . come here."

And she was in his arms and his mouth was sealed against hers while her pulse thrummed in her ears. She yanked at his knotted tie and undid the collar button and two or three others, all the while parrying with his restless, wicked tongue. His hands skimmed her ribs and the sides of her breasts. Although his touch was feather-light, she felt it in her very core. His lips strolled down the curve of her neck to her shoulder and finally to the shadow between her breasts. The tip of his tongue lapped at the skin there, making her tremble. She was so preoccupied by the sensations swimming through her that she hardly noticed when he deftly unzipped the back of her dress. He slipped his hands inside, caressing her warm skin, stroking her lacy bra. The next mouth-to-mouth kiss went straight to her knees, and she leaned back weakly against the kitchen counter and grabbed his shoulders to keep upright.

He tugged the tie from around his collar and flung it aside. Between the two of them, they finished unbuttoning his shirt and sent it flying from his body. Next, the top of her white dress drooped to her waist and his hands cupped her lace-covered breasts. His thumbs worried her nipples. Blaire unfastened the front closure and the strapless bra fell away. She offered herself to him.

Ruben stared at her creamy breasts for a few heart-stopping moments, hardly believing his good fortune. The crests were dark rose. Her soft skin was milky white and so delicate that he could see faint blue veins. He bent his head and took one nipple into his mouth. Blaire jerked spasmodically and moaned with delight. She buried her fingers in his hair and held him against her, but there was no need. He wasn't going anywhere now that he'd tasted her.

"Sweet," he murmured, moving to her other breast. "So sweet."

Blaire arched her spine and closed her eyes to explore an inner heaven. She'd known her nipples were sensitive, but she hadn't realized that expert manipulation could send her reeling through a series of miniature climaxes. Each insistent tug of Ruben's skillful lips released a spear of bright pleasure through her. Her inner thighs tingled, and a heaviness invaded the lower part of her body.

His lips left her breasts and returned to her mouth. This time his kiss told her exactly what the rest of him wanted. His tongue made several brief, plunging forays into her mouth while he unfastened his trousers. The release of the zipper sounded loud and wonderful, echoing off the tiled kitchen walls. The rustle of their clothing, the thumps of her shoes leaving her feet and the whisper of her satin panties slipping down her legs added to the thrill of it all. Half undressed, she wrapped her arms around his neck and rubbed her breasts against the texture of his hair-darkened chest.

His hands cupped beneath her hips and lifted her to perch on the edge of the counter. Blaire kissed him with total abandon and chanted his name. Her desire for him was so acute she was left speechless with hunger. But again, he seemed to know, to sense her body's desperation. He made her wait only long enough for him to slip on protection, and then she felt him enter her.

Ruben thrusted a few times before he climaxed. He then bowed his head and kissed Blaire's shoulder, the curve of her neck, her short chin, her giving, glorious lips. His arms trembled from the strain of holding her weight, and he let her slide down his body, her heels stroking the backs of his thighs, tickling behind his knees, then sliding off his calves. She stood up, clinging to him, her breathing labored, her breasts moving against him.

"Well, what it lacked in finesse, it made up for in sheer, unadulterated lust," he said, smiling. With a sigh of regret, he moved away from her and looked down into her face. Her eyes were closed, her cheeks flushed. "Earth to Blaire, Earth to Blaire."

Her lips curved into a lazy smile. "Don't bother me. I want to savor this. I want it to last and last."

"Uh, Blaire?" He leaned his forehead against hers. "Blaire?" he repeated until her lids finally drifted up to reveal limpid green eyes. "Now that we've christened the kitchen, so to speak, what say we anoint your bedroom next?"

"Next?" She swallowed hard. "You mean, there's more on today's menu?"

He laughed. "Blaire, m'love, we've just tasted the first offering in a seven-course feast." He delivered a sliding kiss down the bridge of her nose. "Come on." He wrapped his arms around her waist and gathered her against his chest. Her bare feet dangled inches from the floor. "You *are* still hungry, aren't you?"

She smiled against his firm lips. "Famished."

9

IN BLAIRE'S BEDROOM, they removed the rest of their clothing and slipped between cool sheets. A night-light provided an amber glow that skated over their skin as they stroked and kissed each other. The sounds of their kisses and murmurs were as arousing to Blaire as were the actual caresses. By the time they'd made their way to the bed, she was trembling with leashed passion.

It had been so long since Blaire had slept with a man that she felt awkward, but Ruben's soft kisses instilled her with confidence. He made her feel special, and she had no doubt that she was wanted—wanted more than she'd ever been wanted by any other man. Jimmy had certainly not gazed at her with such blatant hunger, even on their honeymoon. Jimmy had never been so full of need for her, or her for him, that they hadn't been able to wait until they were both undressed and in bed before they made love. Maybe that's why their love-making had been so perfunctory, she realized. Jimmy had never spent much time arousing her, and the whole deed was usually done within ten minutes or so, leaving her unsatisfied, unfulfilled.

But with Ruben, everything was different. Everything.

Blaire decided to let herself go and give herself completely to Ruben's expert ministrations. This time, lust didn't overpower them as it had in the kitchen. This time, there were no excuses. For a moment, Blaire felt a spasm of embarrassment. After all, the party guests had been gone less than an hour before she and Ruben had fallen on each other like deprived souls seeking sustenance. Ruben's touch put an end to her musings, and revived, but not satiated, they seized the next minutes to explore, investigate and savor.

Ruben luxuriated in covering her delicate body with his. He shifted to one hip so that the mattress took most of his weight. He grinned at his own reaction, shaking his head in resignation.

"What? Am I doing something wrong?"

"No, kitten." He left a plucking kiss on her parted lips. "I'm putty in your hands, do you know that? I don't think you could possibly do anything wrong at this minute. God, Blaire, you are a beauty." Her lashes were long and plentiful, golden with sable tips. They framed eyes that changed from the color of new leaves to deep olive green with her varied moods. At the moment they were . . . kittenish green, sexy green.

"The lack of light in this room must be flattering. I'm no beauty."

"I disagree. Lighting has nothing to do with it." He kissed the tip of her nose.

She made a face and met his sharp gaze. "You don't have to flatter me, Ruben. I'm a sure thing." She gasped when his expression hardened, and she realized she'd offended him. Blaire rested one hand along the side of his face. "Ruben, please, I didn't mean...bad joke, bad timing. I always manage to louse things up. I'm sorry, really sorry. Please, don't let my big mouth spoil—"

The rest of her apology was lost when his lips closed on hers.

He tangled his fingers in the silkiness of her hair. Her lips opened under his, and her tongue danced across his front teeth. He slanted his mouth over hers and touched the tip of his tongue to hers. She made a sound in her throat and he delved deeper, tickling the sensitive roof of her mouth. When he lifted his head, she opened glazed eyes and her breath soughed through her open lips.

"You are, without a doubt, the best kisser I've ever known...personally." She meant every word of it. Kissing had always been arousing for her, but Ruben was lifting it to a new art form. His tongue's suggestive overtures sent messages to every other part of her body.

"Just remember that I can only be as good as my partner," he murmured, his lips leaving a trail of heat on her throat, her shoulder, her collarbone.

Is that a line? Did he say that to those other women? The unwelcome questions deflated the pleasure of his caresses. She shut out the untimely voice, refusing to spoil this night of seduction. All that mattered was the Ruben in her arms, not the Ruben who had earned money by entertaining lonely ladies. He had shed that phase of his life and so should she. *Let it go,* she told herself. *Let it go.*

Thankfully, Ruben's tongue-strokes across her nipples sent all rational thought up in smoke. He kissed his way across her stomach, moving aside the sheet to admire her. Fully aroused again, he drew out the minutes, intent on giving Blaire every pleasure he could possibly bestow. He splayed his fingers across her ribs and nuzzled her navel, then moved lower. She tensed and breathed in his name. He assured her with caressing hands and didn't allow her sharp intake of breath to deter him.

He loved her with his mouth, delighting in her virginal utterances of wonder and halfhearted chastisement. Kissing her inner thighs caused her to sigh with pleasure. Stroking her intimately touched off shudders and moans. He teased and laved her with his tongue, and she gasped and called out his name, her voice all husky and trembly. He loved it. Every hearthammering moment of it.

Blaire drifted down from an ecstasy she'd never experienced before. The cloud of sensual pleasure began to disperse, leaving her mind clear, her vision sharp. She stared down her body at the crown of Ruben's dark head. She reached for him, her hands bracketing his face, and he moved to meet her. She kissed him, lightly, joyously.

"If I could bottle you, I'd be a billionaire," she whispered.

She wanted to reciprocate, so she urged him onto his back. When he realized what she intended, he lay back and closed his eyes, smiling lazily, knowingly. Her hands scouted the territory of him, exploring his warm, firm flesh and patches of soft, curling hair. She sowed seedling kisses down the length of his arms, even in his inner elbows where his pulse leaped against her lips. His hands received special attention. She outlined each finger with the flat of her tongue and branded his palms with hot, flicking lashes.

Sitting across his ankles, she gifted his long, muscled legs with a careful, ardent massage, inching toward his thighs until she could bend her head and let her blond hair fan over his lap. She shook her head so her hair swept across him in a feathery caress. She saw his reaction in the bobbing of his erection. Kissing him there made him groan her name and sent a tremor from his shoulders to his toes.

"Ah, luv, I can't...not when you do that." He reached out blindly toward the bedside table where he'd tossed a foil pouch.

Blaire took matters into her own hands and sheathed him, all the while caressing him, kissing him, murmuring platitudes that made him grin and writhe with anticipation. When she slipped her hand between his thighs he gripped her shoulders and executed a maneuver so practiced and perfect that she found herself lying beneath him before she could even blink. He reached down and guided himself into her, his back bowed, his head flung back in ecstasy. The cords in his neck, his shoulders, his brawny arms, went taut. His desire for her was so beautiful Blaire fought back tears.

He thrust into her, pulled back, surged forward. Blaire gripped his hips and let him take her higher, to that passionate fulfillment.

"S'wonderful, s'wonderful," Ruben whispered, the final vestiges of his raging climax shimmering through him.

Burying his face in the curve of her shoulder, he relaxed gradually, his panting breaths slowing to languid sighs. He wanted to shower Blaire with kisses and thank her for giving him the sweet treasure of her body, her heart, her very soul. He was certain of one thing—it had been a long, *long* time since he'd taken such pleasure from lovemaking. More than pleasure. Joy! Mind-blowing, heart-stopping, sweet ecstasy.

She stirred and he lifted his head. Her hair lay in silky disarray over the pillow. Ruben combed it with his fingertips and fluffed her wispy bangs. He kissed her nose, her pink lips.

"If it's ever been that good for you before, I don't want to know about it," he whispered in her ear, his tongue smoothing along the outer shell. She giggled and squirmed.

"It's never been this good, so don't fret." She sandwiched his face in her hands and kissed him deeply, devotedly. "Promise you won't get mad or take this the wrong way?" He nodded. "Whatever they paid you, it wasn't nearly enough." Before he could react, she kissed him again, engaging his mouth in a sensual excursion that left him breathless and wanting more. "Oh, Ruben. You can't put a price on what we just experienced together."

"So true. There is, of course, one major difference in being with them and being with you. I never wanted any of those women so badly that my fantasies about them kept me awake at night. And if I was fortunate enough to drop off to sleep, those fantasies didn't awaken me in a cold sweat and a desperate need."

"Ruben," she breathed, feeling her cheeks warm in embarrassment but loving every word he spoke. "I had no idea."

"Yes, and that made it even worse. That you were completely unaffected while I was going around with a stiff lap—"

"I wasn't completely unaffected," she interrupted, walking her fingers across his shoulder and down to the bend of his arm.

"Oh, no?"

"No." She looked up at him. "I endured a night or two of steamy dreams." She wrinkled her nose. "In fact, I was awake once or twice when you took a midnight shower. At the time, I thought it was odd that you showered at such a late hour. Now I think I know why."

"The why was you," he said in a growl. "Vamp, vixen, libido-tickler!"

"Guilty as charged," she said, snuggling into a more comfortable position against him. Their bodies fit like interlocking pieces of a puzzle. That she was in bed with him was a marvel in itself! Not in her wildest dreams had she ever thought she'd become intimate with a man she'd met a week ago! She pursed her lips at her uncharacteristic behavior.

"What are you thinking about?" he prodded, shifting to one side to relieve her of his weight.

"How short a time we've known each other and yet I feel...I feel so close to you, Ruben. I feel that I've really gotten to know you. I think you know me pretty well, too. It's weird."

"It's kismet," he said, flinging off the straggling sheet and standing up in all his naked glory. "And it's time for a shower." He wiggled his eyebrows suggestively. "Care to join me, my lovely?"

She smiled up at him and imitated his accent. "Sounds loverly."

He grabbed her hands and hauled her out of bed. "Go get the water warm and I'll be right in."

"Where are you going?" she asked as he jogged from the room.

"Be right back," he called over his shoulder.

Blaire walked slowly toward the bathroom, resisting the urge to follow him. What was he doing? Splashing on more after-shave? Combing his hair? Before a shower? When he padded back into the room again, he threw her a chiding glance.

"I don't hear water running," he scolded, then dropped another foil package onto the nightstand. "Just in case we need it."

Blaire grinned and crooked a finger at him as she retreated into the bathroom. "We'll need it," she assured him, then squealed playfully when he lunged for her.

BRUSHING THE SOLES of her feet against Ruben's hair-silky stomach, Blaire was content to watch sunlight and shadow dapple his skin. The newspaper he held in front of him cheated her of a view of his face, but she found the rest of his body fascinating. She had draped a sheet over most of her body, but he'd exercised no such modesty. She was glad. Her gaze skipped over muscled thighs, lean hips, taut stomach. She memorized the scars on his body, mostly from scrapes and scuffles, she guessed. He looked as if he'd had surgery on his knee and had had his appendix removed.

Smiling, she recalled the night of lovemaking, the lazy massage they gave to each other, and the final, exhausting sexual union before dawn tinted the sky pale pink. They'd slept in each other's arms, their limbs entangled, her head tucked under his chin. Ruben had roused her with kisses just after nine o'clock. He'd been concerned about Molly's next scheduled appearance.

"Don't worry," she'd told him. "I'm supposed to pick her up at Cathy's after lunch." She'd laughed at his relief, and they'd fallen back to sleep.

When she'd awakened an hour later, Ruben had fetched the morning newspaper, brewed coffee, warmed croissants, sliced strawberries and added a few chilled blueberries. They'd turned the bed into a brunch table. Blaire lifted the now-empty tray and set it on the floor.

"Will you look at this," Ruben mumbled to himself from behind the newspaper.

"What are you reading?"

"Hmm?" He peeked around the paper. "Oh, there's an ad here for the restaurant equipment in that place I wanted to lease from Lawrence."

"An ad to sell it?"

"Yes."

"Mr. Lawrence doesn't own that stuff?"

"Nope. The previous renter does. Did you ever eat at that place?"

"Yes, it was mediocre."

"That's what I figured. Mediocrity doesn't cut it in today's restaurant business. Even with fast-food, it'd better be top drawer or you won't last."

She smiled. Oh, she could picture his restaurant. Chic, sophisticated. If he lavished on his diners the same attention he lavished on his lovers, they'd be beating down the door for reservations.

"Bloody good equipment, it is," Ruben grumbled. "Just the thing for what I needed, and it's all there ready to use."

"Why don't you call about it?"

"Why? I've no place to put the stuff if I could buy it. It was perfect when I thought I was going to lease the building, but now . . ."

"Won't hurt to call. Maybe you can offer a down payment and they'll hold it for you until you can find another place to lease."

"That might be months from now."

"And it might be days, weeks." She pressed her heels against him and curled her toes into the springy hair. "Go on! Call and quit sulking!"

He heaved a weary sigh, folded the newspaper and reached for the phone. "Nag, nag, nag." He grinned as he dialed the number, drumming his fingers on her thigh. "Yes, I'm inquiring about the equipment you have listed for sale in the newspaper. . . ."

Blaire went into the bathroom, closing the door. She brushed her teeth and washed her face, giving Ruben plenty of time to complete his telephone conversation. Shrugging into an emerald-green robe, she belted it at the waist and rattled the glass knob before opening the door. The newspaper hid his face from her again. She took her place beside him amid the wrinkled sheets. His expression was a mask of mystery.

"Okay, so what happened?" Blaire smoothed one hand over his chest. "Good news or bad?"

"He won't hold the equipment. It's a dog-eat-dog world out there, kitten. Nobody's interested in doing the other guy a favor. Not where money's concerned." He made a fuss about turning to the sports pages. "If Earla hadn't pulled that stunt, everything would have worked out fine. I can't believe she's so vindictive. It's not like her."

"She's trying to get your attention."

"She's trying to be a first-class bitch, and she's succeeding admirably."

Blaire couldn't help but laugh. She tugged playfully at the hair on his chest, and he snapped his teeth at her like a wolf. "Don't be so hard on her, Ruben. Losing you would be quite a blow."

"Think so?"

"I'll find out soon enough. By the end of the week your job here will be finished and you'll be—"

"Let's not talk about that now." He folded the newspaper and dropped it to the floor. Turning onto his side, he embraced her and one hand found its way inside her robe to cup her breast. "I hope Molly enjoyed her slumber party half as much as we've enjoyed ours."

She laughed against his throat. "Ruben, could you buy that equipment? I mean, do you have enough put back—"

"Yes, I could. But storing it would be too costly for me, Blaire. Besides, as I pointed out, I might have to store the stuff for months. It could wipe me out."

"You could put it in my garage!" She raised her head from his shoulder. "It'll be big enough if I don't park my car in it."

"Blaire, there's too much heavy equipment. Freezers, refrigerators, stoves, ovens, cabinets, the works. They would fill two garages the size of yours."

"Oh." She rested her chin on his shoulder for a few seconds of deep thought. "Hey, what if I give you a glowing letter of reference? I could call Caymen Lawrence and the man with the restaurant equipment and sing your praises to high heaven."

"Thanks, but it's too late for that. Besides, what kind of recommendation could you give? 'Oh, he's great in bed! A wonderful kisser! What the man can do with his tongue down under is positively wicked!'" He chuckled when she gently hammered him with her fist.

"I could recommend you as a butler."

"Which has little to do with my being a successful restaurateur."

"What will you do now?"

He swept his thumb over the crest of her breast and felt it bead. "Snuggle here with you until you have to go get Molly."

"No, I mean, what will you do about your restaurant plans?"

"Oh, that." He tried to sound bored with the subject, but actually he'd been wondering the same thing. What would he do now that his master plan had gone up in flames? No, that wasn't exactly right. He could still succeed, but with a different timetable. "I'll scout for another restaurant location and hope the landlord isn't as finicky about who he leases to."

"What if Dad gave you a reference? That would carry clout, wouldn't it? He's a retired police officer with a sterling reputation."

"Blaire, Blaire!" He smiled and gave her a gentle shaking. "Stop! Let me take care of my future, okay? You don't have to do anything."

"But I want to. I want you to be happy."

"I am happy," he assured her. "I want to swing this restaurant deal by myself, Blaire. I don't want any favors from you. You've done enough. More than you'll ever know."

"What have I done?" She nestled her index fingers in his shallow dimples. His morning beard scraped her fingertips. His arms around her waist tightened, and she felt his firm heat against her belly.

"You've accepted me. You've let me into your home and your heart. That means so much to me, Blaire. Remember when you spilled that milk all over the front of me?"

She laughed and nodded. "How could I forget?"

"I knew then I was in big trouble. One touch from you and I was a goner, kitten."

"You make it sound like death!"

"No, rebirth." He took her mouth in that way she'd begun to crave. "When do you have to pick up Molly?"

"We have time," she said.

"Good. Then let's—" He whispered a suggestion in her ear that made her gasp, then nod eagerly.

10

AFTER STOWING THE VACUUM in the hall closet, Ruben returned to the living room to admire his handiwork. The place sparkled, and the faint aroma of potpourri scented the air. He brushed his hands together in a gesture of accomplishment.

"Damn, I'm good."

Since he hadn't done a blessed thing Sunday except enjoy Blaire's and Molly's company, he had felt guilty and had promised Blaire he'd get back to butlering on Monday morning, which he had. Of course, there was no getting back to what had been normal for them. Still, he didn't want to shirk his duties. He'd signed a contract with Silent Butler and he intended to honor it.

Besides, he owed it to Silent Butler. If the company hadn't hired him, he would have never fallen under the spell of Blaire Thomlin. The week was turning into one of the happiest in his life. By day, he was butler to the Thomlin girls, but at night, he was Blaire's lover. Monday night, she'd tiptoed into his room around eleven and they'd made quiet, inspired love. Blaire had returned to her room before dawn. Tuesday night, he'd visited her room, making love to her and holding her in his arms until early morning. Last night, they'd necked on the sofa after Molly had gone to bed, then they'd taken a stroll on the beach. The full moon reflecting off the restless surf had added to their romantic feelings, and they'd hurried back to the house and into Blaire's bedroom to partake of the sweet release reserved for lovers. Wednesday had been more of the same. They'd taken a midnight shower, making love in the tiled cubicle and again in Blaire's bed. Thankfully, Molly was a sound sleeper and rarely awoke during the night.

Every time he made love to Blaire, his belief that he'd found a partner for the rest of his life solidified. She hadn't asked him any more questions about his short stint as an escort, and for that he was thankful. He wanted to put it behind him and concentrate on loving Blaire. His gaze moved over the sparkle of sunlight on the patio's smudge-free glass door. The throw pillows on the sofa were artfully plumped and arranged. Fresh spring flowers crowned a crystal rose bowl. Now he could attack the kitchen and whip up a fabulous dinner for "his girls."

Grinning, he started for the kitchen, but the chiming doorbell detoured him. Answering the summons, he sucked in a noisy breath.

"Earla!"

Earla Nivens shifted her weight from one suede pump to the other, and the silk folds of her print dress rearranged themselves over her high breasts and rounded hips. She tossed her head in a gesture Ruben had become familiar with, and her waist-long curtain of black hair swished. Ebony and mother-of-pearl combs held her hair back from her temples. A matching antique ring graced her left hand, and a diamond the size of a postage stamp flashed on the right one. She regarded him with eyes the color of rich cocoa. She clutched a suede pocketbook and jingled her car keys. He realized she was as nervous as a sinner at confession. Ruben propped one hand high up on the edge of the open door and stared her down.

"Aren't you going to invite me in?" she snapped.

"If you wanted me to throw out the welcome mat, you should have called first. Have you come around to pull out the knife that you plunged into my back?"

She huffed a sigh. "I don't usually allow *domestics* to speak to me in such a manner." Before he could roar at her, she smiled brightly. "Lighten up, Rube darling. I've been a bad girl, and now I'm being paid back in spades!"

"How so?"

"Let me in and I'll tell you. I'm not going to beg out on this . . . this . . ." She glanced around and curled her upper lip. "This stoop." Then she hit his chest with the back of her hand and waltzed into the foyer. "How long will the little woman be away?"

"Another hour, I suppose. It's her week to car pool and—" He narrowed his eyes suspiciously. "How'd you know Blaire wasn't here?"

"Her car isn't in the garage."

He nodded. "She and her daughter are going shopping for school supplies after they've driven the other kids home."

"Good, that should give me enough time."

Ruben closed the front door and leaned back against it. "Time for what?" he asked warily.

Earla gave one of her deep-throated, closed-lip laughs. "Wary of little ol' me?" She sauntered into the living room and surveyed it with critical eyes. "Small, isn't it?"

"Easy to keep clean," he rejoined. "And homey. I like it."

She arched one charcoal brow. "All good things come to an end. Especially where you're concerned." She waved a dismissing hand. "But I didn't come here to sort through dirty laundry."

"What *did* you come here for?"

"May I sit down, please?"

He felt a sense of betrayal having her here in Blaire's home, but he motioned toward the grouping of sofa and easy chairs. "Please, be Blaire's guest."

"I would have called and arranged a meeting somewhere else, but I suspected you'd hang up the minute you heard my voice." She sat on the sofa.

"You suspected wrong. I'm not that rude or that juvenile."

She looked up and smiled. "You are a gent, aren't you?" Averting her gaze, she busied herself with stuffing the car keys into the small, stylish pocketbook. "My mistake was in sharing you with my friends. But how was I to know how dear you'd become to me?" Her laugh sounded lonely, rueful. It tore at Ruben's heart. "Don't be mad at me, Rube. I had a lot more trouble getting over you than you had getting over me." Folding her hands on top of the pocketbook in her lap, she straightened and surveyed the room again. "Looks like you landed on your feet . . . as usual. Julia Vandermeter said she saw you at the market with the contest winner. Julia says she's rather attractive."

"Julia Vandermeter misled you. She's a knockout."

Earla's gaze sharpened, and she examined him with quickened interest. "Ruben Crosscroft, have you fallen for her?"

He ran his hands down the legs of his jeans and then sat near her on the sofa. Telling Earla what was in his heart before he'd told Blaire was a betrayal he wouldn't commit. "Earla, I don't want any more trouble from you. Let's just shake and let bygones be bygones." He held out his hand, but Earla turned her face away from him to admire the flower arrangement. When she faced him again, Ruben was surprised to see the shimmer of tears in her eyes. "Earla, what's wrong?"

"I'm a sore loser." She shrugged, sniffed and tossed her head. The ends of her coal-black hair brushed the sofa cushion at her hips. "Look, darling, I'm in a jam, and I need one last favor."

"Pardon me while I gape stupidly," he said, sarcasm tightening his throat. "You want a favor from me after the stunt you pulled?"

"I was a bad girl."

"Beyond that, Earla. You know how much my owning my own place means to me."

She swallowed and stroked her suede pocketbook. "I'll make you a deal, darling. You do me this favor and I'll make sure that Mr. Caymen Lawrence leases you the building you have your heart set on."

"The damage you've done won't be so easily erased. I wanted the equipment in it, too, but the man who owns that stuff listed it for sale last weekend. I noticed he didn't run the ad after Monday, so I suppose he sold it all. Now I'll have to round up all those things at an inflated price, I imagine."

"Did you keep his number?"

"I jotted it down somewhere."

"Call him and see if it's sold. If not, you can buy it today."

"Earla . . ."

"Look, I promise to undo the damage. It's not the end of the world, darling. Will you do me the favor?"

Ruben lounged back on the sofa and wondered what emergency had befallen Earla to send her groveling to St. Augustine. "Let's hear it."

"I want you to come back to the Oasis—"

"No, Earla. I told you on the phone when you called last week that I wasn't coming back and I—"

"Yes, darling, I know what you told me. Just hear me out before you start shaking your head, won't you?" When she was sure he wasn't going to interrupt, she continued, "I want you to come back to the Oasis *temporarily*. Just for the weekend. Do you recall what's going on this weekend at the restaurant?"

He sorted through his memory, but came up empty. "No. What?"

"The chamber of commerce banquet is Saturday night, and the mayor's reelection fund-raiser is Sunday evening."

"Ah, so it is." He nodded, remembering how excited Earla had been to land two such prestigious affairs. She'd been anxious that they'd been scheduled for the same weekend, but turning either down would have been unthinkable. "I take it you're shorthanded?"

She released a harsh laugh. "That, darling, is an understatement. As of yesterday, I don't have a head chef."

"What happened to Maurice?" Ruben asked.

"That temperamental French pastry threw a squawling fit yesterday, flung his apron and hat at me, and walked out. When I scheduled both of these wingdings, he swore to me he could handle them without breaking a sweat, and now he's history."

"What about Cornwall?" Ruben asked.

"Cornwall? The junior chef?" Earla looked at him as if he'd gone mad. "Cecil Cornwall thinks New England clam chowder is gourmet cooking. Do you really think he could handle ginger chicken rolls or king crab cakes? I shudder to imagine it!" She had begun breathing quickly during her tirade. "As you can see, I'm quite agitated." She glanced toward the dining room. "Does the little mother keep any liquor around?"

"She does, but it's for her guests, and since you're my...guest," he said, hesitating on that word, "I can't very well serve it to you. It wouldn't be proper."

"My, my!" Earla swept him with condescending eyes. "Aren't we sounding *domestic?*"

"Until Saturday morning, I am."

"What about water? Would you begrudge me that, too?"

Ruben rolled his eyes, but pushed to his feet and went to fetch her some. When he returned with the water, she'd left the sofa and stood looking out through the patio doors. Taking the glass from him, she thanked him with a smile.

"How far to the beach?"

"Just over that rise."

"Nice location." She drank some of the water, then turned pleading eyes on him. "Be my chef for the weekend, Rube, and I swear I'll right all the wrongs I've caused. You'll have your equipment and your lease agreement." She rocked onto one hip, shifting closer to him. "I thought about borrowing one of my chefs from one of my other restaurants, but it's going to be a busy weekend for my other places, too. Please, Rube? You scratch my back and...?" She lifted one hand and lightly scraped her fingernails down the side of his face, then gave his cheek a little pat. "God, I've missed you." Her fingers curled around his chin, and he recognized the slumberous gleam in her eyes.

Ruben gripped her wrist and brought her hand away from his face. "Earla, I'm taken."

The corners of her mouth trembled slightly, and she wrenched her wrist from his grasp. "What's that mean?"

"It means I'm no longer on the market."

"Who's the lucky...not the little mother!"

"Her name is Blaire, and she's special to me." He made sure each word was spoken with the right degree of sincerity, and he knew he'd convinced her when moisture clouded her eyes and she turned her back on him to stare out the patio door.

"She works fast... or was this your doing? Did you sweep the poor dear off her feet?"

"It was a bolt out of the blue for both of us."

Earla fidgeted with her pocketbook and tossed her head, regaining her composure. "Goody for you. So, what's it going to be, Rube? Do we have a deal?" She held out one hand with a look of carefully maintained calm.

He grimaced. "Guess so, mate." He shook on it, but held her hand when she started to pull away. "Friends again, Earla? We can still be friends, don't you think?"

"I don't know." She stared into his eyes. "I'm not sure I'm ready to give up on us being more than that. I have to know I'm good and beat before I cry uncle."

He released her hand. "I can't get to the Oasis before Saturday afternoon, so Cornwall will have to shop for me."

"Saturday afternoon?" she wailed.

"I'll have to rent a car and drive—"

"I'll send the plane for you. There's an airstrip not more than a mile from here. A taxi will take you, and the plane will be waiting. Say, eight o'clock, or can you get away before that?"

He smiled. Rapping commands was so like her. "Earla, I have to hang around for the company to take pictures Saturday morning. They promised to release me of my final duties by noon."

"Pictures?" she asked, clearly exasperated. "Pictures of what?"

"Of me and Blaire."

"Whatever for?"

"Publicity. I'm contest winnings, and Blaire and Molly are the big winners."

Earla tossed her head again and made a disparaging face at him. "What a fine job you landed for yourself, Rube darling. Tell me, what's it like being the jackpot prize?"

"Not bad, really. In fact, it's been the best two weeks of my life so far."

She walked her fingers up his chest. "Even better than the two weeks we spent in Coral Gables?"

He didn't want to hurt her feelings unnecessarily, so he decided not to answer that leading question. "I'll give you a shopping list for Cornwall. Tell him to make his selections with quality, not price, in mind." He released her hand and turned away to locate a pad and pen.

"Of course. You always were terribly good at spending other people's money."

He looked around quickly. "Is this how it's going to be?" he demanded, gripping her chin in one hand when she averted her gaze. "Is it? You're going to take bites out of me every time you don't get your way? Okay, but be forewarned, Earla. I know your vulnerable spots, too, and I won't hesitate next time to tear a chunk out of you." He released her, and she blinked in surprise at his outburst. "Don't mess with me, Earla. You forget I'm not one of those pantywaist yes-men you're so fond of keeping on your payroll. I never was."

She glared at him, but her anger quickly subsided and her shoulders slumped. "You're right. That's why I miss you so, I guess. You never took any guff from me."

"That's not entirely true. I took some, but I never liked it." He squared his shoulders. "Anyway, tell me what you had in mind and we'll select the menu, then I'll jot down a shopping list for Cornwall."

"Fine." She followed him into the dining room and sat at the table while he rummaged through the desk drawer. "Would the little woman object to us having a cup of tea? I'll be glad to leave a donation for her grocery fund."

Ruben tossed a pad and pen onto the table. "Sounds good." He grinned at her attempt to rile him. "And it's on me this time, Earla. You get busy on the menu, and I'll be back in a jiff with the tea. I'll even spring for some Oreo cookies."

"Goody," she replied, drolly, with a regal tilt of her head. "The little mother's version of champagne and oysters?"

He laughed his way into the kitchen.

AFTER FINDING A VACANT bench, Blaire and Jimmy sat side by side and watched Molly and her best friend, Cathy, ride the shopping mall's carousel. When Blaire had pulled in front of the school to pick up Molly and the others in the car pool, she'd been surprised by Jimmy's appearance. He'd asked to come along for the ride.

Blaire offered him more popcorn, and he plunged one hand into the bag. When he brought the popcorn to his mouth, a few kernels fell, landing between his expensive leather sports shoes.

"Are you leaving soon, Jimmy?" Blaire asked, tired of waiting for him to come out and say it.

He smiled, but didn't look at her. "You know me so well. Too well." He finally glanced at her. "Yeah, I'm leaving tomorrow morning early. How'd you guess?"

Blaire shrugged. "You never could say goodbye. It sticks in your throat." She refrained from adding that the phone call from a woman on Molly's birthday had also entered into her deduction.

"I should be used to this, Blaire. Lord knows I've said goodbye enough in my life already."

"Where you headed? Back to Texas?"

"Nope. I've got a six-fifteen flight to Seattle."

"Seattle?" Blaire whistled. "Talk about going from one corner of the United States to the other! Did you get that job?"

"Yep. I'm going to do public relations for the football team there. It's not a coaching job, but I think I'll do all right. The coaching positions I've been offered stink. High schools mostly." He made a disparaging sound. "Insults! Maybe I'm not Joe Montana, but I did play pro ball, and I'm not teaching a bunch of teenagers the game for peanuts."

"Sounds like you've rehearsed that speech. Have you been lecturing yourself or somebody else?"

"Both." He sighed and rested one arm along the back of the bench. "There's this woman in Texas . . . she's principal of a high school and she's been really pushing for me to take the coaching job there."

"But it doesn't interest you?"

"Right."

"The job or the woman?"

He grinned lopsidedly. "The job. The woman isn't half bad. She says I'm no spring chicken and that I should settle down."

"Well, she's right about that," Blaire conceded. "Neither one of us is getting any younger. We have to think about the future, Jimmy."

"Hell, I know all that, but there's just so much planning a person can do before it starts being downright boring to even be alive." He waved at Molly as she went around astride a gold pony with a lavender mane and saddle. "This woman in Texas is a fine gal. Good-looking, sharp, makes decent money, but she doesn't ever surprise me. You know?" He shot Blaire a glance and chuckled. "What am I saying? You don't like surprises as I recall, but I thrive on them. Doing the right thing is great most of the time, but once in a while, you just got to do what your gut tells you to do. My gut knots up when I think about settling down in Texas as high school football coach."

"What does it do when your thoughts turn to Seattle?"

He grinned boyishly. "It tingles. I get kind of scared thinking of trying to charm the public, make them buy tickets, get the press to cover all the attractive stories and refrain from reporting on the blemishes. I've never done anything like it before. It's something different. Makes me nervous. Keeps me on edge. I like that feeling, Blaire. Sitting on the shelf is safe, but it's a sorry existence."

Blaire watched Molly change mounts, this time scrambling onto a black stallion with a silver mane and red saddle. "Well, you can do that kind of thing, Jimmy. You have only yourself to consider." She congratulated herself for not adding that this had *always* been so—and had been one of the major problems in their rocky marriage.

Jimmy reached for the popcorn again. "You're talking about Molly, I guess."

"Yes, I have to consider her above all else." She handed the bag to him and wiped her salty fingers on a paper napkin.

"Above all else?" he asked, clearly unbelieving. "Nobody expects such a sacrifice. Even Molly wouldn't want to know that you look at it that way. You don't really believe it."

"I do believe it, Jimmy. I consider Molly first in everything—"

"If you did, then you wouldn't have divorced me. You believe in family. You think a child deserves a mother and daddy. I know you do, Blaire."

"Well, of course . . ."

"But you divorced me."

"You cheated on me over and over again!"

"And I was wrong to do that. I should have been honest and told you that I couldn't control my roving eye. Nevertheless, when you divorced me, you weren't thinking about Molly having a father and mother under the same roof. Your decision was selfish, Blaire."

"It was forced on me. And it was difficult! I didn't just . . . just throw in the towel and say that's it! I agonized over what to do. I simply couldn't live day in and day out wondering who had been sleeping with my man."

"Hey, hey," he murmured, his arm looping around her shoulders in a quick squeeze. "I'm not blaming you for anything. You did the right thing," he said slowly and with emphasis. "Unhappy parents make for an unhappy child. You and I both know that. What I'm trying to say is we don't have control over every aspect of our lives and we can't plan for every pitfall. I figure I'm doing the right thing for me by taking the PR job and saying ta-ta to Texas. Maybe it's not the most stable choice or the most lucrative offer, but it's the one that will make me happy."

Blaire twisted around to face him. "Jimmy, you sound all grown-up!"

He laughed with her, not taking offense. "Not *all* grown up, but I've gained a little wisdom through the years." He leaned forward to whisper, "Did I mention the former centerfold model who works in the PR department?"

Blaire leaned back and eyed him with reproach. "No, you didn't, but I should have known there'd be a woman in this to sweeten the deal."

"She is sweet." He grinned. "The gal's got some kind of chest on her."

"You sexist." Blaire poked him in the side with her elbow, then picked up the two shopping bags of school supplies she'd bought for Molly. "Well, I think you'll be great as a public relations rep. You've got the smile and the personality for it."

"Thanks, hon. Hey, Blaire, while we're alone, tell me something."

"What?"

"You serious about your butler or what?"

At Jimmy's slow grin, heat bathed her throat and face, then warmed her skin even more when he chuckled.

"Well, I'll be damned. I wondered who would finally make you blush and get all hot and bothered. I never figured someone like Crosscroft would flip your switch." He laughed and dabbed at the corners of his eyes with his knuckles. "The butler did it!"

"Hush!" Blaire glanced around nervously. Molly waved at her and she waved back. "Jimmy, quit braying like a donkey."

"Okay, okay." He made a valiant attempt to curb his guffaws. "So, are you two gonna tie the knot or live in sin?"

Blaire fidgeted with her shoulder bag. "I've only known him a short while and . . . well, it's just too soon to even discuss anything permanent."

"Is he going to move in temporarily or what?" He jutted out his jaw when she glared at him. "I've got a right to know if he's going to be living with you, don't I?"

"Not really."

"He'll be living with *my* daughter, too."

Blaire sighed. "See what I mean? You tell me I should make myself happy, but now you're saying I owe you confidential, private information because of Molly. You can have a harem and you don't tell me squat, but I have one suitor, and you want to know his intentions and how far our relationship has progressed!"

"It's a *relationship* is it? Gone that far already?"

Blaire stood up abruptly. "I'm not going to discuss this with you. I've made my point."

"Yes, you have." He got slowly to his feet, then stepped in front of her, blocking her view of the carousel. "Do you love him, Blaire?"

She stared at the third button of his shirt for several moments. "Yes." She whispered the word past her dry lips. Jimmy cupped her chin in his hand and angled her gaze up to his. His expression was kind, rather than judgmental as she'd expected.

"He's lucky. Hope he knows that. You're a good woman, Blaire. A good wife and mother."

Blaire sucked in a breath, surprised by his admission.

"I never came out and said it like that before, but I always felt it. Guess I had to get some distance before I could admit that you didn't drive me toward other women. I was my own chauffeur." He dropped his hand. "I noticed at the party that Crosscroft is good with Molly. She seems to like him a lot."

"Yes. They get on well."

He shoved his hands in his trouser pockets. "I won't be able to see much of her once I'm in Seattle. It's a hell of a long flight."

"Maybe she can visit in the summer after you're settled in."

"I'd like that. You wouldn't mind too much?"

Blaire laid a hand lightly on his chest. "She's your daughter, too, and always will be, Jimmy. No matter what or who comes into my life, nothing will change that. I hope you'll be happy in Seattle."

Jimmy clasped her hand and brought it to his lips for a brief kiss. "You be happy, Blaire. The next time around, you grab an old boy who'll not only be a good father to Molly, but who will make your heart do a little jig every time he walks into the room. You deserve it." He faced the carousel and draped an arm around Blaire's shoulders. Molly's laughing chatter drifted to them. "Hell, we all deserve it."

Through a misting of tears, Blaire looked up at Jimmy's profile. For a few fleeting moments, she saw the man she'd fallen in love with years ago.

11

JUGGLING SHOPPING BAGS while trying to bat aside the two helium balloons Jimmy had insisted on buying Molly at the mall, Blaire tried to grasp the front doorknob.

"Molly, get those things out of my face," she snapped, frustrated, and her daughter jerked aside the balloons. "Thank you." She twisted the knob and the door eased open on oiled hinges.

"We're home, Ruben!" Molly called, skipping ahead and trailing her heart-shaped airships. "Look what Daddy bought me at the ma—oh, sorry. I thought you were alone."

"That's okay, Molly m'love. Hey, those are pretty, but they don't look like school supplies to me."

Blaire dropped the shopping bags in the foyer and moved cautiously toward the dining room. One look at the attractive woman sitting next to Ruben at the table was all Blaire needed to identify the visitor. Earla Nivens had come to collect her property.

"There you are!" Ruben almost lunged at her, and Blaire wondered if he was overjoyed to see her because she'd rescued him or because he felt guilty. "Blaire Thomlin, this is Earla Nivens. Earla, Blaire and Molly, my current employers."

Blaire wished she could force back time a few minutes to give herself a chance to brush her hair and repair her makeup. Self-consciousness stole through her, and she couldn't help running her fingers through her hair. The other woman didn't miss the sign of vulnerability.

"Looks like you've had yourself quite a day," Earla said, rising to show off her wrinkle-free designer dress. "Thank you for allowing me to turn your dining room into a temporary office. Rube and I had some business details to iron out." Her gaze flickered over Blaire's one-piece sunsuit and grass-stained tennis shoes.

"Sure, that's okay." Blaire forced herself to face Ruben. "Since you're discussing *business,* Molly and I will make ourselves scarce."

"We're finished." Ruben glanced at Earla. "Aren't we?"

"No, not really. I wanted to confer with you about what I need to do to get you back on your feet."

"Oh, right." He looked from Earla to Blaire with a hint of desperation. "Let me get Blaire and Molly settled and I'll—"

"We can settle ourselves, Ruben," Blaire interrupted, pressing a hand against the back of Molly's head and herding her from the dining room. "You go ahead and . . . entertain your guest."

"I'll start dinner—"

"No need. Jimmy is taking us out." The sound of a car door slamming drifted into the house. "That'll be him now. Nice to meet you, Mrs. Nivens."

"Nice to meet you," Molly parroted.

"Come on, Molly. Let's not keep your dad waiting. And leave those balloons here. If they hit me in the face once more, I swear I'm going to sink my fingernails into them."

"Okay, okay," Molly grumbled, tying the strings to the leg of the coffee table in the living room. "You sure are grumpy."

Blaire wrestled her brush from her purse and passed it through her hair several times. "Let's go."

"But I thought we were going to change clothes."

"I'm too hungry." Blaire opened the door to Jimmy. "Mind if we go somewhere casual?"

"No, that's fine with me," Jimmy said, leaning down to lift Molly into his arms. "Okay with you, Mol?"

"Pizza?" Molly suggested.

"Sounds great." Blaire reached back inside to grab the knob and close the door behind them, but froze when Ruben came into view. His dark, glowering expression unnerved her. She jerked back her hand as he strode toward her. He nodded a curt greeting to Jimmy.

"What time will you be back, Blaire?"

Blaire shrugged. "Hard to say."

Jimmy lowered his brows and examined the two tense adults carefully. "I'll have them home around eight," he told Ruben. "I've got an early flight out of here tomorrow."

"Oh, so you're leaving?"

"That's right." Jimmy grinned. "Now, don't you go getting the blues over that piece of news." He gave a jocular salute and chuckled. "Good luck, pal."

Blaire linked her arm in Jimmy's and flinched when Ruben closed the door with unnecessary force. Molly looked from the door to Blaire.

"Mom, are you mad because that woman is visiting Ruben?"

"Woman? What woman?" Jimmy asked, shifting Molly from one hip to the other.

"Some woman Ruben knows. I forget her name."

"I'm not mad about anything," Blaire said, moving ahead of them toward the rented car. Jimmy reached past her to open the passenger door, and she felt his breath warm the side of her neck as he bent close.

"Liar, liar, pants on fire," he taunted.

"Oh, shut up," Blaire grumbled, but the teasing brought a smile to her. "How does pepperoni with extra cheese sound?"

"Sounds like you're changing the subject," Jimmy drawled, helping Molly fasten the back seat safety belt. "But pepperoni it is."

HOURS LATER, PULLING her feet up onto her chair, Blaire took a few moments to sort through Ruben's explanation of Earla's visit. One inevitability took precedence.

"So you'll be leaving for Palm Beach Saturday?"

Sprawled on the sofa, one hair-darkened leg draped over the back of it, Ruben peeked from under the arm that covered his eyes. "Yes, but not until after the company has taken its photos of us."

"Oh, right, I forgot about that." She frowned, dreading the necessity of smiling for the camera while her heart cracked open. "Shouldn't take long and then you can be on your way."

Ruben lowered his arm and sat up, his movements exaggerated, snaillike. He brought his gaze to meet hers. His eyes were darkly blue and damning. "Do you think you're the only one with feelings around this place, Blaire?"

"I don't know what you mean by—"

"Earla offered me a sweet deal and I took her up on it. That doesn't change my feelings for you one iota."

She stared at him. Words were inadequate to convey her jumbled feelings.

"I thought you'd be happy for me." He propped his elbows on his knees, and his hands hung loosely between them. His brief shorts and tank top left most of his body bared to her admiring gaze. "I've patched up things with Earla, and there's no hard feelings. Blaire . . ." He spread out his hands in a beseeching gesture. "Talk to me!"

Blaire hugged her knees tightly against the ache in her abdomen that had begun early that morning and had increased throughout the long, confusing day. "It hurts that you'd accept her offer to help after throwing mine back in my face." There, it was out. No matter that she sounded irrational. It galled her that Earla could change from villain to vindicator in one fateful afternoon.

"I didn't throw your offer in your face," he objected in a singsong voice.

"I offered to supply a letter of recommendation and you refused it. But your old flame offers and you call it a sweet deal."

He cursed and ran a hand down his face. "Blaire, don't be like this. If you'd stow the jealousy for a minute, you'd see that Earla's recommendation will hold more weight with Lawrence than yours ever could. It means the world to me, but wouldn't mean beans to Lawrence."

"Why is it that everyone around here thinks I'm riddled with jealousy? Huh?" She stuck out her chin. "I simply think it's unsettling how quickly you jumped on that woman's offer. She throws a monkey wrench in your plans, ruins everything, then waltzes in and asks a favor and you lose your memory!"

He rocketed to his feet and paced in front of her. "Did you hear anything I just said?"

"Yes, so you needn't yell. You'll wake Molly."

He bit his lower lip until his temper subsided and he could speak civilly again. He faced her and was struck by both her beauty and his fury at her. "Blaire, she's going to square things with Lawrence. She's the one who loused up the deal for me, so I think it's only fair that she be the one to set things to right again. I don't understand why you refuse to see that."

"She also talked you into coming back to Palm Beach to work for her."

"Temporarily. She's in a bind. She needs me."

Me, too. The words branded Blaire's tongue, but she managed to keep them to herself. Uncurling her body, she straightened slowly and rose from the chair. "I've got to take some aspirin."

"What's wrong?" He was immediately solicitous, his tone of voice changing from hard-edged to soft concern. One hand caressed the sleeve of her silky robe from shoulder to cuff. "Headache?"

"No."

"What, then?"

"Guess."

Ruben cleared his throat and the tips of his ears flushed pink. "Oh, that. When did you get it?"

"This morning. I've felt achy and out of sorts all day."

"And Earla's surprise visit didn't help."

"No, it didn't." She went to the kitchen for the bottle of aspirin she kept on the windowsill over the sink. The cap spun uselessly and Blaire cursed.

"Here, let me." Ruben took the bottle from her and loosened the child-proof cap. He grasped one of her hands, turned it palm up, and tapped out two aspirin. "There you go."

Blaire tossed the pills to the back of her throat and washed them down with water. Bracing her hands on the rim of the sink, she gave into the urge to let her head roll to relieve the tense muscles in her neck. The circular massage of Ruben's fingers at the base of her neck was welcome relief, and she didn't move away from him.

"I've got an idea," he whispered, his lips brushing against her skin. "Plug in your heating pad and lie down on it, then I'll give you a massage that's guaranteed to ease menstrual cramps." He gave her a love bite on her shoulder when she shook her head. "Just do it." He slapped her backside playfully and gave her a gentle push toward the archway. "I'll be there in a minute."

Blaire didn't have the energy to protest, so she went to her bedroom and tugged the heating pad from beneath her bras and panties in the dresser drawer. She plugged it in and then slipped out of her robe. She lay on her stomach on the pad, wearing only panties and a shortie nightgown of lemon-colored satin, and closed her eyes as the heat increased.

Ruben entered the room and closed the door quietly behind him. He started for the bed, but stopped in his tracks, his gaze riveted to the alluring body awaiting him. His fingers tightened around the bottle of lotion and vial of oil he'd located in the bathroom. God, she was beautiful! Smooth golden legs tempted his gaze, and he followed their length from her toes to her thighs. Her shortie nightdress was hiked up on one side to reveal a taut buttock, scantily covered by a wedge of pink bikini panties. He felt himself growing hard.

Blaire raised her head and looked back at him. "I'm not asleep."

"Good." He smiled, telling himself to get a grip. "But you will be soon." Lifting the bottle and vial, he wiggled them at her. "You're going to love this, sweetheart."

She gave him a wan smile, then laid her head back down on the pillow and closed her eyes. "The heating pad feels great."

"Do you have bad cramps every month?"

"Not usually."

"Hope you're okay."

"It's nothing. I've been on the run all day and...well, I'm just tired." Her breath caught in her throat when Ruben's lotion-slicked hands wrapped around the back of her neck. "Mmm, that's nice."

"That's nothing," he promised, frowning at the thin straps of her nightie. He tried pushing them aside. "Blaire, take this thing off so that I can get at you."

A sliver of panic passed through her. "Can't you just...Ruben!" He'd grabbed the hem of her nightie and pulled it up to her shoulders. In the next instant he swept it over her head and she found herself naked, except for her bikini panties.

"That's better." He warmed a pool of lotion in his hands and eyed the golden expanse of her back and the curve of her waist. "Much better." He rubbed his hands together, then placed them on Blaire's shoulders.

He set to work to loosen each bunched muscle with his thumbs and the heels of his hands. She murmured with pleasure as he continued his expert massage. The way he was sitting on the side of the bed was awkward. Chancing the return of her uneasiness, he kicked off his sandals and straddled her, his thighs pressed against hers. She looked back at him. Evidently, what she saw didn't threaten her because she settled down and closed her eyes again.

His thumbs inched down her spine. He spread his fingers, curving them around her waist, and added pressure against the small of her back. She moaned appreciatively as he made tiny circles with his thumbs. He oiled his hands with the jasmine-scented liquid. His slick fingers kneaded her lower back and hips and slipped beneath her to administer relief to her abdomen. The skin there was hot, the heating pad warm against his hands. Her long sigh encouraged him. Grasping her shoulder, he rolled her onto her back. She offered no resistance, not even opening her eyes. Ruben was glad because it afforded him the unselfconscious pleasure of admiring her body.

Blaire could feel the heat of his gaze as keenly as she'd felt the warmth of the electric pad. She kept her eyes closed, not willing to confront him. The massage had melted her muscles to liquid, her will to putty. She wanted to keep it that way and indulge herself for a while. The tingling ache moved up her body to her breasts. Soon she could no longer separate the ache of her muscles from the ache of her desire.

His slick, warm hands covered her cool breasts, and Blaire whimpered and squeezed her eyes even more tightly shut.

"Blaire? Did I hurt you then?"

"No, no." She shook her head. "My breasts...they're tender."

"I'm sorry." He lifted his hands off her, but she grasped his wrists and brought them back to the fullness of her.

"It's okay. I l-like it." She swallowed and lifted her lashes just enough to see his slow grin. As she watched, he moved to straddle her again, his buttocks settling lightly upon her upper thighs. He still wore his cutoffs and tank top, and Blaire wished he were naked. She closed her eyes, alarmed by her own lustful inclinations. She was having her period, for heaven's sake! She'd never wanted to make love during those few days each month. She'd never felt particularly sexy during that time. But here she was breathless, her body thrumming with anticipation, her heart pounding, her chest tense with passion. She let her hands slip to her sides, giving him free rein.

His fingers moved like trickles of warm water down her breasts to her stomach. He massaged her tenderly, soothing the aching muscles, chasing away the dull throb. Blaire floated on the edge of sleep, but was brought back to vital awareness by the slick wetness of Ruben's mouth on her breast. He tongued her, and she wove the fingers of one hand through his thick, wavy hair.

He made a stiff point with his tongue and teased the pearly nipple. He kissed his way to her other breast and took that pink crest between his thumb and finger, squeezing gently. Blaire writhed beneath him, and he felt her thighs move apart. He stretched out on top of her, kissing her breasts with increased ardor, caressing her waist and hips with slick, oiled hands. He liked the whisper of his hairy thighs against her smooth ones. He liked the smell of jasmine on her skin. He liked the way her nipples responded to the touch of his tongue, the suckling of his lips. Most of all, he liked the way her pelvis thrust against him in a silent cry.

He inched his fingers under the waistband of her panties and into the soft, curling hair. She thrust against him again, her head moving from side to side, her hair spilling over the pillow. His fingers touched, went deeper, rubbed the kernel of flesh that was already hard and pulsing. She cried out his name and he felt his own sex lengthen, thicken, press against the fly of his shorts.

"Ruben . . . Ruben . . . we can't." She twisted her face into the pillow and flung one arm across her middle. "I can't. Not now." Her green eyes implored him. "Please understand. I want to, but . . . I . . ."

He placed a finger to her lips. "It's okay, kitten. I understand." And he did, but one part of his body wasn't as understanding. He lifted himself from her, moving stiffly, uncomfortably. Gently, he guided her onto the heating pad again, then spread a light blanket over her. He kissed her temple. "Good night, kitten."

"Good night. Thanks for being so sweet to me, Ruben. And thanks for the massage. It was . . . well, thanks."

He picked up his sandals and padded barefoot to the door. He paused a moment to savor the fan of golden hair spreading across the pillow behind her and the perfection of her profile. It was with profound regret that he left her to her dreams.

THE ONSLAUGHT of her cycle and the spicy pizza she'd eaten turned out to be a horrible combination. By morning Blaire felt queasy. By afternoon she'd visited the bathroom five times. By the time Molly got home from school, Blaire was in bed with the heating pad again.

"Mom, are you going to be okay?" Molly asked, standing beside the bed.

"Yes, sprout." Blaire ran her hand through Molly's short black hair. "I've just got a tummy ache. You know, like when you eat too many sweets and your tummy rebels?" She waited for her daughter's nod. "Well, that's what's happening to me. The pizza upset my stomach."

"It didn't mine."

"You're lucky. Have Ruben give you a snack. You can watch TV, if you want."

"Okay." Molly gave her a kiss. "Mom, today's Ruben's last day."

"Yes, I know. You'll miss him, won't you?"

"Uh-huh."

"But it was fun having him. I'm glad you won the contest."

"Me, too." Molly brightened. "Can I help him pack?"

"Pack?"

"Yeah. He's in his room packing."

Blaire sat up. She felt as if a stake was being driven through her heart. "Wouldn't you rather watch a movie or something?"

Molly shrugged. "I guess. I think *Parent Trap* is on the Disney Channel."

"Let me get you a glass of milk and some cookies." She stood up and went into the kitchen with Molly. After she'd settled Molly in front of the TV with a tray of cookies and milk, Blaire walked cautiously toward the extra bedroom . . . Ruben's room.

Standing on the threshold, she stared at the open suitcases on the bed and chewed on her lower lip to keep from sobbing. Ruben moved into view, his arms full of underwear and socks, which he dropped onto the bed beside the cases. He sensed her presence and jerked around.

"You need anything? How are you feeling?" He grasped her hands lightly and swung them between their bodies.

"I'm feeling a little better."

"Good enough to maybe eat dinner with me and Molly in a few hours?"

"If the food is bland enough, maybe."

"Chicken and rice soup. It'll do you good." He pressed his lips to her forehead. "You feel hot. Do you have a temperature?"

"I don't think so." She stepped closer and buried her face in the curve of his neck. "You're really leaving, aren't you?" Her throat thickened and her misery reached new heights. "When Molly said you were p-packing, I . . . oh, Ruben! I'll miss you so m-much."

He gathered her against him and closed the door behind her. Nuzzling her hair, he let her squeeze him tight, caress his back, kiss his throat.

"I'll miss you, too, kitten," he said into her hair. "But I'll only be in Palm Beach over the weekend. I'll be back in St. Augustine by Monday, and I'll make a beeline for this house, I promise you." When she made no response, he curled one hand beneath her chin and brought her face up to his. "Blaire, say you believe me."

"I believe you," she repeated, but her heart rebelled. She thought of Earla and the more affluent life-style she could give Ruben. She thought of how easy it would be for Ruben to return to that life in Palm Beach. No strings. No rings. Just Mercedes, diamonds, mansions and lonely women. "I never thought you'd pack everything. You could leave your things here."

He smiled. "I'm all packed now. Might as well get this stuff out of your way."

It's not in my way. You're not in my way. She laid her cheek against his chest and listened to the beat of his heart. He held her in a relaxed embrace, his hands clasped at the small of her back. "I hope everything works out for you, Ruben."

He breathed a choice four-letter word and sat her down on the corner of the bed. Squatting before her, he took her hands in his. "Blaire, don't you think I'll miss you? Don't you think you've changed my life forever? I'm going to help Earla out this weekend at the restaurant and that's all. That's all." He nodded his head for emphasis. "Don't act like I'm gone for good. It infuriates me."

Her woebegone expression didn't change. Ruben ground his teeth. Irritation and passion meshed, melted together, fused, fired his blood. He swept the stacks of clothing off the bed and pushed Blaire onto her back. He thrust his hands under her shirt and palmed her breasts through her bra. His mouth slanted over hers. He angled his head and covered her mouth more completely. His tongue wet her lips, stroking again and again until her lips parted and her jaws relaxed. He thrust his tongue deep and she made desperate, sexy sounds. Her hands grasped his shoulders and then slipped over them to stroke his back, his neck, his hair. Her thighs parted to sandwich his. Ruben rocked his hips, his hardness rubbing the heart of her femininity. She groaned and the sound reverberated in his head.

Her hands somehow worked between their bodies to fumble with the buttons of his jeans. One by one, she released them. Her fingers inched inside and were momentarily thwarted by his underwear, but then seeking fingers found turgid flesh. She stroked him and the whole world pulsated around him. Her hand moved up and down the silky heat of him. He groaned, threw back his head, grimaced as ecstasy held him suspended in wondrous agony.

"Blaire, I'm going to...oh, God...I'm going to...I swear." The words tumbled from him, unheeded, unfettered. His hips bucked as he neared his breaking point. Her hand never stopped, never ceased its torrid tempo. He thought he might die. He thought he might not mind it at all. "Blaire, oh, sweet, sweet," he whispered, his voice rasping, barely sounding at all. "Ahhh, ahhh, yes, yes, *yes!*"

"Mom?"

They heard the tapping on the door, but neither could find a voice, a response. Blaire was still in awe at the power she could wield, the pleasure she could give. Ruben was teetering between heaven and earth, gradually becoming conscious of his spent condition.

"Mom? Grand's on the phone for you," Molly yelled through the closed door. "Mom, Grand wants to know if you're feeling better."

Blaire shook herself from her own self-absorption. She mirrored Ruben's slow, wiseacre grin. "Tell Grand I'm feeling *much* better and that I'll call her back later."

"Okay."

They listened to Molly's fading footfalls, then released their pent-up breath and laughed at their predicament. Blaire moved first, slipping off the bed to her feet. She adjusted her clothing and hair.

"I'm going to take a long soak in the bath before dinner."

Ruben nodded. "I'm going to . . . clean up." He glanced down at himself, feeling a bit embarrassed for having completely lost himself in what she was doing to him.

"Ruben?"

"Hmm?" He liked the sexy gleam in her cat eyes.

"How do you feel?"

He grinned. "*Much*, much better."

"Good." She glanced shyly at her toes. "I wish we could . . . I mean, I wish I wasn't green around the gills and that I wasn't in my. . ."

"I know. Me, too."

She left the room. Ruben fell back on the bed and stared at the ceiling. He found himself feeling sorry for Jimmy. To lose this woman, he knew, would leave a hole in a man's heart forever.

12

"ONE MORE PICTURE, and I'll get out of your way. Promise." The photographer offered up a practiced smile. "Now, Ms. Thomlin, could you sit on the couch? Molly, would you sit on your mother's lap? Good. Mr. Crosscroft, with tea tray in hand, could you stand at the side here . . . like that, good. Bend at the waist and offer that tray to them. Wonderful. Everyone stay just like that while I focus. I really appreciate your patience, Ms. Thomlin, what with you feeling ill and all."

Blaire pasted on a smile. Her twenty-four-hour bug had decided to go forty-eight hours. Or maybe she was only reacting to Ruben's imminent departure. Last night they'd held each other in a sweet, agonizing embrace. They'd talked about the inconsequential lives they'd led before their fateful meeting. Sleep had finally claimed them. This morning they'd tiptoed around each other as if they were both made of hairline-fractured glass. Even Molly was in a fractious mood. Blaire hadn't stopped to think how Molly would take Ruben's moving out, but she knew by Molly's uncharacteristic fussiness that her child was on the verge of tears.

The company photographer had arrived right after breakfast and commandeered them into a variety of ridiculous poses. At least, they seemed ridiculous to

Blaire. Mainly because the photographer was treating Ruben like a butler, and Ruben had far exceeded that in her mind and in her heart. In Molly's, too.

"Everybody smile! Mr. Crosscroft, could you lean a little closer to Ms. Thomlin? You're out of the frame. There, that's perfect. Smile. Everybody happy! You're winners!"

The flash popped and recharged with a high-pitched whine.

"Maybe we could do one more with Molly—"

"I'm sorry, but I think twenty pictures is plenty," Blaire said, letting Molly hop off her lap. "We'd like a few minutes to say goodbye to Ruben before he has to leave us."

"Oh, sure. I understand. So, you all became good friends during the two weeks?" The photographer began stowing his equipment into a couple of large cases.

"Yes. Good friends. Molly?" Blaire caught her daughter by the shoulders when she noticed the tears streaming down her face. "What's wrong, sprout?"

"I d-don't want to say goodbye."

"Oh, sprout. Don't cry or I'll start boo-hooing with you." She gathered her daughter to her chest, where her own heart felt bruised and tender.

"Blaire, why don't you see the photographer off and let me take Molly into the kitchen for a glass of juice."

"I don't want any," Molly wailed.

"Come on, Molly. I'd like to talk to you." He gently disengaged Molly from her mother's embrace and forced her gaze up to his. "I promise not to say goodbye, Molly."

Molly sniffed, studied Ruben's serious expression for a few moments, then tucked her hand in his. "Okay." She let him lead her away.

"Cute kid," the photographer said.

"Thanks." Blaire wanted to join the two people she loved instead of having to make small-talk with a stranger. She smoothed wrinkles from the front of her cherry-red skirt. She'd selected the skirt and white shirt with its strawberry motif decorating the collar and button placket because she thought it would look cheerful for the pictures, thus being in direct contrast to how she felt inside. "Sorry I wasn't more cooperative."

"But you were! I know how it is to be under the weather and have to muddle through things like this. You've been more than kind." He snapped the locks on the cases, then patted his jacket pocket. "If you'll just sign this photo release, I'll be history." He extended a fountain pen.

Blaire signed her name on the appropriate line and escorted the photographer to the door. He'd told them his name earlier, but for the life of her she couldn't recall it.

"Goodbye." Blaire winced. God, she hated that word.

"Bye, now." He trundled, cases in hand, to the van parked in her driveway. Blaire waited until he was behind the wheel and the engine had roared to life before she closed the front door and walked quietly toward the kitchen. She could hear the deep rumble of Ruben's voice. As she drew nearer, the rumble became words.

". . . So from this day forward I'll no longer be your butler, Molly, m'love. From this day forward I'll be your friend. Forever. Let's shake on it." He offered his hand across the kitchen table and Molly clasped it. "Okay, now let's high-five on it." He met her hand high in the air with a gentle pop. "Now let's soul-shake on it." He grasped her hand one way, then another. Molly giggled. "Let's high-ten on it." Four hands collided in mid-air. "Now let's hug on it. Come here, you."

Molly charged off the chair and barreled into his waiting arms. He hugged her, closed his eyes, and his face showed the importance of the moment. Blaire blinked away tears and swallowed the lump in her throat. Ruben opened his eyes and noticed her. He tenderly set Molly from him.

"Now, will you let me have a few minutes alone with your mom?"

"Sure." Molly kissed his cheek and whirled around to her mother. "He's not leaving for good, Mom. He'll be back Monday. Can I put on my play clothes now?"

"Yes, but pick out colors that match. No purples and oranges, please. I'm sick to my stomach enough already." Blaire smiled and patted her daughter's rump as she went past her. It was with effort that she brought her gaze to bear on Ruben again. Emotion choked her, tore at her heart, made her tremble.

"Don't look at me like that." He strode forward and pulled her limp body into his arms. "I'll tell you what I told your daughter. I'll be back Monday. Why are you two acting as if I'm going away for good?"

"None of us knows what tomorrow will bring," she said, her voice muffled against his shirt.

"Tomorrow I'll be busier than a one-armed paper-hanger, but come Monday it will all be over and I'll be camped on your doorstep." He cradled her face in his hands. His thumbs swept her cheeks, clearing away the tears. "Tell me you believe me, Blaire. Say it." His mouth flirted with hers. "Say it."

She looked into his eyes and the cloud hovering over her was whisked away. "I believe you."

"Everything's coming up roses, kitten. I'm going to get my restaurant, the equipment, the whole nine yards. You'll see. Come Monday I'll be the happiest chap on earth."

She snuggled into his arms and wished she could take all the credit for his jubilant mood. She wished she didn't have to share it with another woman. A car horn sounded, violating their privacy.

"Bloody hell. That's the taxi Earla arranged to take me to the airport."

Blaire nodded. Earla Nivens was an impatient woman, she thought as she noted the time. Twelve noon. Right on the dot. Ruben Crosscroft was no longer on her clock. He was on Earla's time now.

AGATHA THOMLIN STOOD by the kitchen window and watched her husband push her granddaughter on the swing. She laughed to herself at her husband's broad smile. "He's a sucker for a pretty girl."

"Hmmm?" Blaire turned from the sink where she was dicing celery and carrots for the beef stew simmering on the stove. "What'd you say, Mother?"

"Oh, I was talking to myself. Dex and your daughter are having a fine old time out there. Reminds me of when he'd play outside with you. Dolls, horsey, school, whatever. He'd play for hours and hours without one bit of self-consciousness. Never failed to amaze me." She watched Blaire attack the next carrot with the paring knife. "I told Dex we should stop by today in case Molly needed cheering up. Maybe it's you we should be concerned about."

"Me? Mother, I told you. I had a little bug yesterday, but I'm feeling fine today."

"Has Ruben called you?"

"Ruben? No." She tried to sound nonchalant. "I'm sure his boss lady is keeping him very busy."

Agatha sidled up next to Blaire and angled her head to peer into Blaire's face. "Your eyes are much greener today. Green with jealousy."

"Mother, please." Blaire laughed, but cut it short because the counterfeit noise grated. "There's no need for him to call. He said he'll be back Monday."

"Blaire, let's me and you be straight with each other," Agatha said, leaning back against the counter and crossing her arms. "You need to be honest with someone, so try me. Are you feeling threatened by Earla? Do you sense that Ruben has feelings for this woman? Sexual feelings, that is?"

"I . . . well, he obviously did once."

"Yes, but what about now?"

"I don't know, Mother. He says he doesn't."

"But you feel threatened."

Blaire dumped the vegetables into the stew pot and wiped her hands on her apron. "I don't know. I guess so." She sighed and slumped against the counter, head down, eyes closed. Since yesterday when Ruben had ducked into that taxi Blaire had felt so many things—none of them good. She'd sent Molly out to play, then she'd gone into her bedroom, closed the door, and had a long, self-indulgent cry. Dinner last night had been dismal: tomato soup and grilled cheese sandwiches, eaten while Molly watched television and Blaire stared blindly at the screen. Molly had endured Ruben's departure like a champ. Blaire felt like a wimp, showed up by a nine-year-old optimist.

"Oh, ye of little faith," Agatha quoted with a smile. She took one of Blaire's hands and led her to the kitchen table where they sat side by side in the ladder-backed chairs. "So, is it serious between the two of you?"

Blaire nodded. She plucked a napkin from its holder and folded it into fours. "I feel as if I've never been in love before, Mother. Like it's the first time for me, and I'm not familiar with the rules."

"There are no steadfast ones. They change with the players."

"I guess so." She tore off a strip of the paper napkin, her hands busy, but her mind traveling a different course. "Something Jimmy said the other day started me thinking. . . ."

"Wait. Let me assimilate this." Agatha closed her eyes and rested a hand across her forehead while Blaire looked on in amusement. "Okay. So, you're saying that Jimmy Jacobs said something *thoughtful?* Is that what you're saying?"

Blaire laughed and shook a finger at her mother's sarcasm. "Mother, poor Jimmy has been the brunt of many a joke—"

"Many a *good* joke," Agatha interrupted.

Blaire nodded. "Yes, some of them have been doozies. He's been the brunt of many a good joke for several years. We've been using him as a whipping boy and that's been good for me."

"But enough is enough?"

"Yes. I'm all well, Mother. While we've been sharpening our fangs on Jimmy, he's grown up." Blaire laughed at her mother's dubious expression. "Well, he's not all grown-up, but he's taken on a bit of maturity. He'll never be a responsible person, but he's not completely irresponsible anymore, either."

"What sage bit of advice did he cough up, Blaire?"

"It wasn't really advice. He admonished me for saying that I had to always place Molly's welfare before mine." She realized that she'd shredded the napkin. She scooped up the pieces and tossed them into the trash barrel behind her. "He said there were some circumstances when I should put me first."

"Well, well." Agatha sat back, arms folded. "Jimmy *has* changed."

"Do you agree with him?"

"On that subject, we agree. Sounds to me as if you two buried the hatchet this time around."

"We did. For the first time in a long time I could look at him without wanting to smash his face in."

Laughing, Agatha clasped her hands together dramatically and shook them triumphantly at the ceiling. "Healed at last! Thank God, she's healed at last!" She squeezed one of Blaire's hands. "I'm happy for you, darling. It'll be good for Molly, too. Children pick up on feelings. I'm sure Molly noticed the animosity between you and Jimmy, although you both hid it fairly well."

"He said some things I needed to hear—things that let me off the hook, so to speak. And I returned the favor. It felt so good to just let go of the guilt, the blame. I feel pounds lighter."

The stew began to bubble, and Blaire went to the stove to stir it and reduce the flame. She glanced outside, but her father and Molly weren't in the backyard anymore.

"Guess Dad and Molly went to the beach."

"He brought a kite. They're probably trying it out."

"Molly needs a man around. Dad is great with her, but she needs more. She deserves more."

"Are you thinking about Jimmy or Ruben now?"

Blaire cut open a loaf of French bread. "Ruben, of course. He's so good with Molly, Mother. He's so sweet to her. So gentle."

"I noticed, especially during her birthday party. And it's obvious she thinks he can do no wrong."

"She's smitten. Puppy love, I think." Blaire began buttering the thick slices of bread and placing them on a cookie sheet. "I hope that doesn't present a problem."

"What problem?"

"Well, when she figures out that I'm . . . that Ruben and I are . . . well, that we're involved with each other, she might get upset."

"Blaire, you aren't raising a nincompoop. Molly already knows that you and Ruben are sweethearts."

"How . . . when? She said that to you?"

"Yes, at her birthday party. I said something about Ruben and you getting along nicely, and she told me that you two were boyfriend and girlfriend, as she put it."

Blaire stared at the sheet of bread for a few moments while her mind ironed out this new wrinkle. "Well, I'll be." She laughed softly and shoved the cookie sheet into the warm oven. "We weren't then, you know. I mean, we hadn't done anything. It wasn't until later that we . . . well, you know."

"Slept together?"

Blaire swallowed nervously. "Yes." She felt herself blush more deeply when Agatha laughed at her. "Mother, it's hard to talk to you about this. I'm . . . you're my mother."

"Don't be embarrassed." Agatha patted her hand, reassuringly. "You're still my little girl. Always will be, no matter who you sleep with."

"Mother." Blaire rolled her eyes, but her uneasiness abated. She sat down again. "Another thing that Jimmy said . . ." She smiled, remembering. "He said he hoped I'd fall in love with a guy who makes my heart do a jig. He said I deserved it."

"And is your heart a dancer when Ruben is near?"

"Oh, yes." She closed her eyes. For a moment, she thought she could smell his distinctive after-shave. Bold Hunter. Oh, he was that! "Mother, I've never felt like this before. He makes me feel . . . so much! So many things that I can't even begin to count them."

"You love him."

Blaire shrugged helplessly. "I love him."

Agatha leaned forward and kissed her cheek. "Good for you, darling. Have you two made any future·plans or are you playing it by ear?"

Blaire plucked another napkin from the holder. "We haven't talked about that. We've only known each other a couple of weeks, and everything's happened so fast."

"Blaire, his past isn't causing you problems, is it?" Agatha's flame-colored brows formed a V.

"No. I've come to grips with that."

"Good, because I think that was a fluke. It's not part of his true character."

"Yes, I agree. Still . . ." She tore a long piece off the napkin. "He's back in Palm Beach. Back with her."

"But it's different now. He has you and Molly. He's only doing the woman a favor so that she'll help him get his restaurant instead of spoiling everything like she did before."

"I offered to help him and he refused me." She wadded up the napkin and threw it into the barrel. "Earla offers and he starts packing his bags." Blaire rescued the bread from the oven before it burned. She barely noticed the scrumptious aroma.

"Oh, those eyes are green now," Agatha taunted. "Cat fight!" She hissed and fashioned her hands into claws. "Are you going to do this every time he has business with a woman?"

"It's not like that, Mother. Earla was a bad influence on him. You said yourself that it seemed out of character for him to be an escort—a gigolo." She forced that word past dry lips. "But he did it for her. He stopped listening to his heart and listened to her. Why couldn't the same thing happen again? After all, she was here for an hour or so and had him ready to move back to Palm Beach."

"Blaire, he's there for the weekend working. Don't make a tempest in a teacup."

"It stings that he'd accept her help over mine."

"It makes sense to me. She's the one who queered his deal in the first place. She should be the one to clean up the mess she made. Once this weekend is over, he'll be through with her. You just watch. Mother knows best."

Blaire finished transferring the hot bread from the baking sheet to a basket. She turned to face Agatha. "Mother, if he shows up Monday, I'm going to grab him and never let him go again. I swear it."

"Good for you, darling." Agatha grasped her shoulders and stood toe-to-toe with her. "But what's this 'if' business? Don't you believe a man when he tells you he loves you and that he'll come back to you?"

Blaire laughed at her own insecurity. "Yes, I believe him. He loves me. I know he loves me."

Suddenly, Agatha pulled Blaire close for a long, heartfelt hug. Blaire smiled, surprised by the gesture.

"Mother, what's this for?"

"I'm thrilled for you, Blaire." Agatha held her at arm's length. "When I first laid eyes on Ruben Crosscroft, I thought he was exceptional. I'm so glad you think so, too. For a while, I was afraid you'd throw him out on his ear because of that business in Palm Beach. I'm so relieved that you looked past all that to the heart of him. He's a dear man, and he loves you. That means so much. Jimmy never worshiped you, never adored you. He loved you, yes, but that's not enough for the long haul. When Ruben looks at you, it's there in his eyes and in his smile, and he doesn't give a darn who sees it. I saw the way he looked at you during Molly's party. Such longing, such devotion! To have a man feel that way about you, Blaire." Agatha fetched up a sigh. "Oh, it's a blessing."

The sound of the patio door sliding open and Dex and Molly's chattering interrupted the mother-daughter exchange.

"Is lunch ready yet?" Dex called from the other room. "We've worked up quite an appetite!"

"Soup's on," Agatha answered, but she held her daughter's gaze for a moment longer.

Blaire kissed her mother's soft cheek. "We're both blessed, Mother."

13

"Hello?"

"You have a sexy voice, kitten."

Smiling, Blaire closed her eyes and let Ruben's voice coddle her ear, her mind, her heart.

"You still there? It's Ruben."

"I recognize your voice," she said, laughing. "Did you think I'd hung up on this obscene phone call?"

"If you think this is obscene, then hang on, kitten. I'm so needy that I can hardly keep my mind on anything but you and what I'd like to be doing to you."

"Ruben," she breathed, feeling a twinge of longing corkscrew through her midsection. "Where are you? I'll come pick you up." Last night she'd slept fitfully, her mind churning with anticipation of Monday morning. She had watched it dawn, fixed herself a pot of coffee, and then spent the morning and early afternoon waiting for the phone to ring or the front bell to chime. She laughed at her own behavior. "You should have seen me attack this phone when it *finally* rang. Because of you I haven't done one bit of work. All I've done is daydream about you and me. So, tell me. Where are you?"

"I'm glad you've missed me."

"I have. How did the work go?"

"Everything turned out fine. The compliments rained down. I even tried out a new dish—crab-stuffed baked tomatoes—and it was a big hit. People couldn't get enough of it."

"I'm so glad. Ruben, hearing your voice isn't enough. I want to see you, hold you."

"Blaire . . ." His sigh breathed across the line.

Blaire tensed. Bad news, she thought. He's calling with bad news.

"I'm not in St. Augustine yet."

"Oh." Relief weakened her knees. "You called to tell me you're leaving now?" She glanced at her watch. "You'll be here by dinner. That's perfect." She looked around at the crepe paper and banner. "Molly will be so happy. She's missed you almost as much as—"

"No, kitten. Listen, I'm going to stay here a few more days."

Blaire's knees gave way and she sat on the sofa. Her spirits drooped around her like a smothering cloak.

"Earla hired a new chef, and she asked if I'd stay on a few more days until he gets acquainted with the routine around here. I know how hard it is to be thrown into a strange city and a strange kitchen, so I've taken pity on the poor chap and I've agreed to show him around. You know, where the best markets are, who's the best butcher, which dishes are favorites in these parts."

"Couldn't Earla or the junior chef instruct him on those things?"

"Yes, but I agreed to help out. Earla's been a gem. Lawrence has come around. He's having his attorney draw up a lease, Blaire. And that equipment . . . you remember that restaurant equipment I wanted?"

"Yes." She closed her eyes and fat tears rolled from the corners.

"He didn't get a buyer for the whole package, and he said he'd wait until next week before he advertised to sell it piece by piece. I'll have a lease agreement by then, and I can go ahead and buy the equipment. All of it. Isn't that great, Blaire?"

She cleared her throat. "It's wonderful news, Ruben. I can understand how you feel beholden to Earla."

"Blaire, she's really been helpful. You do understand, don't you? I'll phone you again after I know for sure when I'll be leaving here."

"Yes. That'll be fine." Sobs threatened to steal her voice. "I've got to go now, Ruben. Thanks for calling."

"Blaire, are you all right with this?"

"Sure. Someone's at the door. Got to go. Goodbye, Ruben." She swallowed hard. "Goodbye." She replaced the receiver, dropping it into the cradle as if it suddenly burned her hand. Her gaze drifted up to the banner swinging gaily from the living room archway.

Crushed by disappointment and angry that her knight had fallen off his horse and into the arms of another woman, Blaire propelled herself from the sofa. She reached up, grasped the center of the banner and gave a vicious jerk. The paper tore in half. Blaire charged on to the dining room where candles stood in tall brass holders, waiting for the strike of a match, and china and crystal glinted. With one swipe of her arm, Blaire sent the candles flying off the table and to the floor. She plucked artfully arranged linen napkins from the plates and threw them at the helium balloons tied to the backs of the chairs.

Sobbing, she headed for the kitchen to switch off the burners under the roast and vegetables. She turned off the oven where a cake sat, half-baked. Wilting into the nearest chair, Blaire hid her face in her hands and let the tears come. The telephone rang, but she ignored it. She knew it was him, and she had nothing else to say. Her last goodbye had said it all.

RUBEN LISTENED to the mechanical rattling at the other end of the line and drummed his fingers on the desktop. "Answer the phone, Blaire," he urged, but she didn't. He knew she was home. He'd just spoken to her. "Blaire, answer the blasted phone!"

He slammed the receiver into the cradle and ran both hands through his hair. His imagination painted a picture of her, distraught, angry with him, furious that he'd break his word to her. Hell, and why not? He was furious with himself! Stupid to think she'd take the news well, that she'd be understanding. Oh, she'd tried. She'd said the right words, but he could decipher the pain in her voice. It tore at his heart. Pleasing her had become important to him. Her pleasure was far more important than his own. When that had happened, he couldn't say. Maybe when he'd gotten his first good look at those incredible eyes of hers—green and warm and so full of life. Or maybe when he kissed her and felt all the promise stored in her delicate, lovely body.

If he could only make her believe that he wasn't deserting her. All he was asking for was a few days—three, perhaps four—and then he'd be back in her loving arms. If she'd take him. That last goodbye had fallen like hail upon him. She wasn't serious, was she? Could she really turn him away because of this one broken promise? His common sense told him he could win her back. What was eating at him was that he'd hurt her, disillusioned her. His armor was tarnished, and it bugged the hell out of him.

"Rube?"

Ruben jerked around. Earla stood just inside the office. He'd come into the manager's private office to use the phone. He propped his elbows on the desk again and washed his face with his palms.

"Uncle."

He sighed. "What?"

"Uncle," she repeated. She strolled toward the desk.

"Earla, I'm not in the mood to play games. Uncle who?"

"Not who, darling. I told you that I wasn't ready to cry 'uncle' where you're concerned." She tapped her long fingernails on the edge of the desk. They were the same shade as her lipstick. "I give. I surrender. Uncle!"

He fell back in the plush executive chair and stared at her. Her gesture was lost on him. He'd given up on her months ago and considered them finished, over, kaput.

"I had thought there might be a chance I could lure you back into my life," Earla explained. "But I saw your face just now and realized I didn't have a snowball's chance in hell." She came around the corner of the desk and perched one shapely hip on the edge, swinging a slim leg and expensively shod foot. "You look as if you've lost your last and best friend, darling. Did she take your news hard?"

"Yes, she did. I promised her I'd be home today. Of course, she's disappointed."

"You never ever looked that way when you disappointed me. You're really in love with her, aren't you?"

He nodded and met her gaze directly. "Completely. For the first and last time in my life."

Earla arched her dark brows and tossed her head. The ends of her hair spread over the schedules and receipts scattered across the desk. "Ruben, you're a romantic! But I should have known that. Only a man with a soft, romantic heart could be so sweet to women. You changed our lives, you know. Me, Bev, Carol and Merrylu. You made us believe in the goodness of men again. One tends to lose faith after bumping up against a few scoundrels. But then someone like you comes along and makes us remember that there are some heroes left in this world."

"I'm no hero. I was paid to be nice."

"Don't be so melodramatic, darling. So you were given money. Big deal. Instead of us buying you bottles of after-shave, sweaters, watches and all the other things women buy men to let them know they're special, you were given cash. Don't make those gifts of friendship sound crude or tawdry."

He reflected for a few moments. "Yes, the money was given freely. I never asked or demanded to be paid."

"That's right. I made the suggestion to Bev that she pay you for your time. She was glad to do it. We knew you had ambitions, and we wanted to help you achieve them while you're young enough to enjoy your successes."

"So what happened, Earla? Why'd you try to ruin my future?"

Earla tossed her head again. "I became more interested in my future, rather than yours. I fell in love with you, Rube darling. I didn't want to share, and I didn't want you leaving me to open your own restaurant. My mistake was in thinking you loved me, too."

Ruben hoisted himself higher in the chair. "Now, Earla, I never said—"

"I know, I know," she interrupted. "You never said you loved me. That's true. My first husband never said it, either, and we were married eight years! I miscalculated with you, that's all. But I still care for you, Rube. Very much."

He ran a finger around his shirt collar and freed the top button. "Earla, you're a nice woman, and I appreciate all you've done."

Her laughter mocked him. "Because I care for you, I'm telling you to hit the road." She shook an index finger to a jazzy beat. "And don'tcha come back no moah, no moah, no moah, no moah."

Ruben smiled and clasped his hands behind his head. "Gee thanks. By the end of the week, I intend to do just that."

"No, not by the end of the week. Now."

"Now? But what about my helping Jacques out until he can—"

She waved aside his question. "I'm paying that Creole chef big money. He ought to be able to find his way around the restaurant kitchen without any help. Cornwall can acquaint him with the local markets and butchers." Noticing Ruben's sharp scrutiny, she colored with uncharacteristic embarrassment. "Okay, so I didn't really need you to hang around here. I cooked up that little story, and it worked."

"Why come clean now?"

"Because I saw you. When she answered the line, I saw your face light up with such . . . oh, it was a sight! I want to make a man smile like that. It was damn near a swoon!"

It was his turn to blush. He ducked his head so that she couldn't see the high color in his cheeks and on the tops of his ears.

"You'll never look at me that way, Rube." Her hip slid off the desk edge. "So get out of here, you lovesick Aussie. I can't stand another minute of your moping around with your heart on your sleeve."

He rose from the chair. "Thanks, Earla. You're a pal."

"I am not. I've never been any man's *pal* and I'm not starting now." She pivoted and moved with a hip-swinging gait to the door.

"Earla, did you know that your new chef is interested in you?" He grinned when she turned to face him again. "He asked if you had a husband or current lover."

She propped one hand high on her left hip. "This may come as a shock to you, Rube, darling, but I don't shack up with every chef I hire," she said lightly.

"I was joking around with him and he told me that his last girlfriend—a twenty-year-old swimsuit model from Los Angeles—gave him an interesting nickname." He waited, confident she would take the bait.

Earla sighed and rolled her eyes. "What nickname did she give Jacques?"

Ruben winked. "Long John." He stepped closer to catch the glint of curiosity in Earla's brown eyes. "And she wasn't referring to his underwear."

A husky, bawdy laugh pushed at Earla's lips. "Ruben, you are bad. So bad you're good." She lifted the hand on her hip to his shoulder. Her fingers dug in for a moment in an affectionate squeeze, then she flicked an imaginary speck from his shirt. "Better get going if you want to get there by nightfall."

"Thanks for everything, Earla."

She shook her head to set her hair swaying. "See you around, Ruben." She became serious. "I hope she knows how lucky she is."

Ruben shook his head. "You've got it wrong, luvvy. I'm the lucky one."

HE RANG THE DOORBELL again, but he knew no one would answer. Blaire's car wasn't in the garage. Ruben stepped off the porch, located the fake rock among the real ones in the flower bed, dug the extra front door key from the niche in its underside, and used it to let himself in.

"Blaire? Molly?" he called, striding through the foyer. A faint fragrance of cooked meat hung in the air, so he headed for the kitchen first. He flipped on the lights as he went.

He lifted the lid off the roaster and stared at the partially cooked meat, its juices congealing around it. A small pot of green beans and another of new potatoes were cold. The oven light was on. Ruben bent over to peer through the thick glass window at the half-baked cake. It had started to rise, then had sunk and dribbled over the sides of the pan. He laid one hand against the outside of the oven. Cold. So she'd been gone for quite a while. Right after his phone call?

In the dining room he picked up a crumpled linen napkin and examined the toppled candles. The helium-filled balloons of red and pink brought a lump to his throat. She'd been planning a big welcome home for him and he'd spoiled it.

But it was the torn banner in the living room that made his throat ache with strong emotion and blurred his vision. Jagged tears through the paper broke the letters into gibberish, but he could see what it had proclaimed: Welcome Home, Ruben!!! Red hearts took the places of the letter *O*s.

"Oh, God." He dropped onto the sofa and held his head in his hands. It didn't take a genius to know what his phone call had interrupted. "I'm so sorry, Blaire. But where are you?" He reached for the phone and dialed a number he'd learned by heart.

"Hello?" Agatha Thomlin answered on the third ring.

"Agatha, this is Ruben Crosscroft."

"Oh, hello."

"Is Blaire there?"

"Blaire? No."

"Molly?"

"No. They're probably at home."

"I'm calling from their home." Disappointment battered him. He knew of nowhere else to call.

"Oh, I see. Was she supposed to meet you there?"

"No. I...I wanted to surprise her, but nobody's here. I thought she might be visiting you and Dex."

"Sorry. I'm sure they'll be home soon."

"Do you know where they might be? Does she have a friend nearby she might be visiting?"

"Ruben, is this an emergency? Can't you wait until she comes home?"

"Yes...I mean, no. It's not an emergency. I just want to see her."

"And I'm sure she wants to see you. Molly has school tomorrow, so they won't stay out late. They probably went out to eat. Without you there to cook for them, they're back to their old routine. Neither Blaire nor Molly wastes much time in the kitchen."

He smiled ruefully. "Yes, I know. Sorry to bother you. If you should hear from her, will you ask her to call me here?"

"Certainly. Welcome back."

He glanced at the ripped banner. "Thanks."

Ruben went out to the car he'd rented at the airport and removed his luggage from the trunk. He brought it inside and started to put it in the guest bedroom, then changed his mind and left it in Blaire's, with the hope she wouldn't throw it and him out the door when she returned. He checked his watch. Seven-thirty. She should be home by eight, he told himself.

By eight-thirty, he revised that thought to nine or ten. At ten he stood at the front windows and stared at the dark street, searching for the flash of headlights. At eleven he started pacing and kept it up until twelve-fifteen. He checked out the phone, making sure it was working. He went outside and walked all around the house. At one-thirty, he took two aspirin and fell onto the sofa, flinging one arm across his eyes to block out the light and help ease his splitting headache. He drifted off to sleep around three in the morning.

At seven he woke up, frantic because Blaire still wasn't home.

"Where in the bloody hell are you?" he demanded, his long legs carrying him from one empty room to the next. He wondered if he should call her parents again, but nixed that. Why worry them? He'd wait. If he hadn't heard from her by noon . . . no, he'd call the school later and check to see if Molly was there. If she was, then that would mean that Blaire was roaming around.

"Come home, damn it!" he bellowed, standing in the center of the living room, fists clenched at his sides, head thrown back, eyes closed.

That's how Blaire found him. The sight of him distraught and disheveled was almost more than she could bear, but her pride held her from him.

"How did you get in here?"

His eyes popped open and relief poured through him. "Blaire! Molly! Thank God! Where have you two been all night? I've been worried sick."

"Ruben!" Molly charged across the room and hugged him around his waist. "We stayed in a hotel last night, but we had to come home early so I could change for school."

Ruben picked Molly up in his arms and kissed her forehead, her cheeks, her hair. He brought one of her small hands to his lips. "Molly, I missed you like crazy. You know that?"

"I missed you, too."

"Molly, come on. Let's get you changed for school and then we'll eat some breakfast. We've got to hurry. Your ride will be here soon." Blaire took Molly from his arms, giving Ruben only a chilly glare. "You didn't tell me how you broke into my house."

"I didn't. I used the spare key in the fake rock outside."

She said nothing, just took Molly with her toward the bedroom wing.

"I'll cook breakfast while you two change," he offered.

"No." Blaire spun around, her face full of pain. "Don't. You aren't the butler anymore. I'll fix breakfast."

"Blaire, I don't mind—"

"I do. Stay out of my kitchen."

"Mom, why are you—"

"Just hush, Molly." Blaire marched out of his sight, but not before Molly sent him a befuddled glance over her mother's shoulder.

WAVING MOLLY OFF to school, Blaire tried to prepare herself for the next confrontation with Ruben. She was mad. Burning, blazing mad. He'd ruined her happy plans, then showed up anyway, acting as if he should be given a hero's welcome. Did he think he could pull strings and make her dance to whatever tune he whistled? Now I'm here, now I'm not. Don't look for me. Boo, surprise! Dance a jig, step off a funeral march. Well, she wasn't his puppet, and she wouldn't allow him to jerk her around anymore! She loved him, but not so much that she'd sacrifice her sanity.

Flattening her hands against her stomach, where butterflies made like kamikaze pilots, she drew in a deep breath before stepping from the foyer into the living room. Ruben sat on the sofa. A magazine lay open in his lap, but he closed it and tossed it aside when he saw her.

"Is it time for my appointment?" he asked, sarcasm and resentment clearly evident.

"Why is your luggage in my bedroom?" she countered with her own brand of the same.

He narrowed his eyes. Here it comes, he thought. He knew he shouldn't have left it in there. Oh, to hell with it! "Because that's where I want my things to be. Your bedroom." He sprang up from the sofa. "When I left here, I thought it would be better if I gave you some breathing room. I told myself to rent an apartment someplace nearby and court you for a period of time. But my weekend away from you proved one thing to me." He thrust his face close to hers. "It proved I was capable of hatching some dumb ideas." He caught her shoulders. "All I could think about was making love to you, Blaire. I don't want to spend another night alone with those thoughts. I've never been so miserable. Not even when I was on that bloody treasure ship for weeks on end with no females in sight."

Blaire shook off his hands. "Did Earla make everything right for you?"

He stuck his hands in the back pockets of his jeans. "Yes. She came through, like I told you on the phone. I'm going to lease the building. Hopefully, I'll be able to open for business in a couple of months." He examined her face. Her eyes darkened with an emotion he couldn't name. "Why did you stay in a hotel last night?"

"Because I wasn't in the mood to face this." She kicked at the torn banner at her feet.

"It was sweet of you to go to so much trouble for—"

"Spare me, please," she drawled, bending to snatch up the pieces of banner. Her fist closed over one heart-shaped *O* and crushed it. "What made you decide to keep your promise? I'm surprised Earla let you."

"Blaire, if you're trying to make me mad, you're succeeding."

"Did you sleep with her?"

The ugly words burst past her lips and made Blaire flinch. Tears sprang to her eyes, but she blinked them aside. She stood her ground, arms crossed, hands clasped around her elbows, chin trembling.

"Do you really think I'm so shallow that I'd leave your bed and crawl into another woman's? Blaire, I love you. Do you hear me? *I'm in love with you.*"

Instead of reassuring her, his proclamation seemed to add to her misery.

"Then why did you turn to her?" she asked, her voice quaking. "That h-hurt so much, Ruben. I offered to help you, but you wouldn't even hear me out. You ran to her. You turned everything over to her and she rescued you. We could have w-worked something out. Why didn't you give me a ch-chance to be your hero-ine?"

"Blimey, Blaire, I didn't . . . come here." He placed a hand gently at the back of her neck and pulled her to him. She pressed her wet face into the curve of his neck. He let her cry, feeling like a heel for bringing it on. But,

Christ! How was he supposed to know his deal with Earla could upset her so? "I'm sorry I didn't refuse her yesterday. I shouldn't have agreed to stay on a few more days after I promised you I'd be back on Monday."

"It made me feel like s-second place."

"That's crazy, Blaire." He tightened his arms around her shoulders and rocked her back and forth. "Kitten, what can I do to make you believe that I'm totally, completely, utterly yours?"

"It's just that she's so attractive and . . . persuasive. I thought she'd talk you into leaving me. You'd packed all your belongings. You didn't have to come back here. Then when you called yesterday, I just knew you were gone forever."

He tipped back his head to stare blindly at the ceiling. He expected this, but he hadn't expected to feel so desolate. Knowing he'd hurt her was almost unbearable.

"I would have loaned you some money to rent a storage building. I would have helped you, Ruben. B-but you wouldn't let me. You l-let her."

The sobbing wasn't lessening. If anything, it was getting worse. Ruben guided Blaire to the sofa and made her sit down with him. He handed her the tissue box.

"Earla was the one who messed everything up by refusing to give me a recommendation. So why shouldn't she pull my fat out of the fire? I thought you understood this."

Blaire made angry swipes across her eyes with the tissue. "Well, I don't! Why you even *speak* to that woman is beyond me!"

"You're jealous."

"So what if I am? You're a pushover where she's concerned!"

One side of his mouth inched up. "Oh, that's me. A pushover. Round heels. I'm easy pickin's." His eyes rolled dramatically. "But only with you, Blaire. Earla's a friend, but she's out of my life. My life is here with you, I hope."

"You say you love me, but you didn't turn to me when you needed advice or help. You let those other women help you, and you said you didn't even love them."

He placed his hands on his knees and took a deep breath. He *had* to make her understand the peculiarities of being male. "That's right. I don't love them. I don't want to prove anything to them. I don't want their respect, their admiration, their esteem." He twisted sideways and saw the glimmer of comprehension in her eyes. "So, I didn't mind letting them give me a push up the ladder. But I want to be strong for you, Blaire. I want to stand on my own two feet and be a success for you. I want to be your provider, your lover, a man you can depend on. I don't give a damn what those other women think of me, but I care deeply what you think."

She placed one hand alongside his face. He turned his lips into her palm and left a kiss there. Inching closer, he laid one hand on her thigh, bared by her white shorts. Her skin felt warm and satiny smooth.

"I knew you would have given me money, Blaire, but I couldn't accept it after I'd told you about taking money from those other women. I didn't want you to question my motives for *one second*. I couldn't bear it if you'd thought I might be scamming you. I preferred to work things out with Earla or lose out completely than take one cent from you and have you wondering if I might be using you. That's how much your opinion of me matters."

Blaire's throat felt thick, and her voice emerged husky with emotion. "Ruben, I never worried about that with you. When I offered to help, I did so out of love. I wanted to find a solution with you."

"I know." His thumb swept her silky thigh, back and forth. "Guess I'm just your typical Australian macho man. I want to prove myself to my woman."

She leaned closer until her mouth was inches from his. "Ruben, sweetheart, you don't have to prove a thing to me. I'm yours. Oh, God, it's been so lonely without you here." The last word was a mere breath of sound. His mouth covered hers in a kiss that went a long way toward healing her hurt feelings.

"*You* were lonely?" he said between quick, raining kisses. "I've been out of my mind wondering what happened to you. I've got imps with hammers having a ball in my head right now because I didn't get hardly any sleep last night."

"Poor baby," she crooned, then nipped his ear with her teeth.

He whispered her name gruffly and pushed her backward until she was lying flat. He settled over her: a warm, heavy, very male, very sexy blanket. His mouth flirted with the corners of hers. Exasperated, she clamped her hands at the sides of his head and opened her lips over his. He tugged down her tube top until he'd exposed her breasts to his hands' caresses. While his tongue plundered her mouth, his nimble fingers brought the crests of her breasts to rosy readiness. She shifted beneath him and parted her thighs to let him settle more completely against the heart of her desire.

"Blaire, are you still . . . ?" He lifted his face from the pillow of her breast and looked at her with cornflower-blue eyes. "When I left, you were having your—"

"It's over," she said, catching his drift, and so glad to deliver that bit of news. "I finished."

"Thank God!" he said, voicing relief for both of them, then his mouth closed on one distended nipple. "Ah, so sweet. You taste milky." He lapped at her breasts again. "No, you taste like honey." His tongue stroked, making her shiver with longing. "Mmm, kitten, you taste better than any woman has a right to taste."

"Ruben, I love you so much." She wove her fingers in his thick hair, savoring each strand. "I want you to make love to me all morning, then I want you to prepare us a great big lunch—"

"How am I to do that if I'm not allowed in *your* kitchen?"

She smiled jauntily. "I'm giving it back to you as a wedding present."

"A wedding present?" His dark brows arched.

"You will marry me, won't you?"

His brows lowered menacingly. "I'd like to see you try and stop me."

"I won't try. I'll be too busy trying to hold on to you." She crossed her wrists behind his neck and locked her heels against his muscled thighs.

"I'm not going anywhere, and that's a promise." He felt her react to that, giving a little jolt. Slowly, he lifted his mouth from hers to stare down into her sexy green eyes. "Hey, I keep my promises. I promised I'd be here Monday and I was here. Where were you?"

Her sable-tipped lashes drifted down demurely to concede the point. "Okay, okay. You got me."

Ruben slipped his arms beneath her and gathered her more completely against his yearning body. Her hands inched under his T-shirt and her fingernails raked his back. He thickened with desire and she rocked her pelvis forward, nudging him, beckoning him.

"You're so right, kitten," he growled against her seeking, soft mouth. "Mmmm, so-o-o right."

HARLEQUIN *Temptation*

Rebels & Rogues

Quade had played by their rules . . .
now he was making his own.

The Patriot
by Lynn Michaels
Temptation #405, August

All men are not created equal. Some are rough
around the edges. Tough-minded but
tenderhearted. Incredibly sexy. The tempting
fulfillment of every woman's fantasy.

When it's time to fight for what they believe in, to
win that special woman, our Rebels and Rogues are
heroes at heart. Twelve Rebels and Rogues, one
each month in 1992, only from Harlequin
Temptation. Don't miss the upcoming books by
our fabulous authors, including Ruth Jean Dale,
Janice Kaiser and Kelly Street.

WELCOME TO

The quintessential small town where everyone knows everybody else!

Finally, books that capture the pleasure of tuning in to your favorite TV show!

GREAT READING... GREAT SAVINGS... AND A FABULOUS FREE GIFT!

Each book set in Tyler is a self-contained love story; together, the twelve novels stitch the fabric of the community. The covers honor the old American tradition of quilting; each cover depicts a patch of the large Tyler quilt.

With Tyler you can receive a fabulous gift ABSOLUTELY FREE by collecting proofs-of-purchase found in each Tyler book. And use our special Tyler coupons to save on your next TYLER book purchase.

Join your friends at Tyler for the sixth book, SUNSHINE by Pat Warren, available in August.

When Janice Eber becomes a widow, does her husband's friend David provide more than just friendship?

If you missed *Whirlwind* (March), *Bright Hopes* (April), *Wisconsin Wedding* (May), *Monkey Wrench* (June) or *Blazing Star* (July) and would like to order them, send your name, address, zip or postal code, along with a check or money order for $3.99 (please do not send cash) plus 75¢ postage and handling ($1.00 in Canada) for each book ordered, payable to Harlequin Reader Service to:

In the U.S.	In Canada
3010 Walden Avenue	P.O. Box 609
P.O. Box 1325	Fort Erie, Ontario
Buffalo, NY 14269-1325	L2A 5X3

Please specify book title(s) with your order.
Canadian residents add applicable federal and provincial taxes.

TYLER

JAYNE ANN KRENTZ

Dreams
Parts One & Two

The warrior died at her feet, his blood running out of the cave entrance and mingling with the waterfall. With his last breath he cursed the woman—told her that her spirit would remain chained in the cave forever until a child was created and born there....

So goes the ancient legend of the Chained Lady and the curse that bound her throughout the ages—until destiny brought Diana Prentice and Colby Savager together under the influence of forces beyond their understanding. Suddenly they were both haunted by dreams that linked past and present, while their waking hours were filled with danger. Only when Colby, Diana's modern-day warrior, learned to love, could those dark forces be vanquished. Only then could Diana set the Chained Lady free....

BIG SUMMER READ

Summer Reading At Its Best

In July, Harlequin and Silhouette bring readers the Big Summer Read Program. Heat up your summer with these four exciting new novels by top Harlequin and Silhouette authors.

SOMEWHERE IN TIME by Barbara Bretton
YESTERDAY COMES TOMORROW by Rebecca Flanders
A DAY IN APRIL by Mary Lynn Baxter
LOVE CHILD by Patricia Coughlin

From time travel to fame and fortune, this program offers something for everyone.

Available at your favorite retail outlet.

BSR

Back by Popular Demand

Janet Dailey
Americana

Janet Dailey takes you on a romantic tour of
America through fifty favorite Harlequin
Presents novels, each one set in a different
state, and researched by Janet and her husband,
Bill.

A journey of a lifetime. The perfect collectable
series!

August titles   #37 OREGON
       To Tell the Truth

       #38 PENNSYLVANIA
       The Thawing of Mara

OFFICIAL RULES • MILLION DOLLAR MATCH 3 SWEEPSTAKES
NO PURCHASE OR OBLIGATION NECESSARY TO ENTER

To enter, follow the directions published. If the "Match 3" Game Card is missing, hand print your name and address on a 3"×5" card and mail to either: Harlequin "Match 3," 3010 Walden Ave., P.O. Box 1867, Buffalo, NY 14269-1867 or Harlequin "Match 3," P.O. Box 609, Fort Erie, Ontario L2A 5X3, and we will assign your Sweepstakes numbers. (Limit: one entry per envelope.) For eligibility, entries must be received no later than March 31, 1994 and be sent via first-class mail. No liability is assumed for printing errors, lost, late or misdirected entries.

Upon receipt of entry, Sweepstakes numbers will be assigned. To determine winners, Sweepstakes numbers will be compared against a list of randomly preselected prizewinning numbers. In the event all prizes are not claimed via the return of prizewinning numbers, random drawings will be held from among all other entries received to award unclaimed prizes.

Prizewinners will be determined no later than May 30, 1994. Selection of winning numbers and random drawings are under the supervision of D.L. Blair, Inc., an independent judging organization, whose decisions are final. One prize to a family or organization. No substitution will be made for any prize, except as offered. Taxes and duties on all prizes are the sole responsibility of winners. Winners will be notified by mail. Chances of winning are determined by the number of entries distributed and received.

Sweepstakes open to persons 18 years of age or older, except employees and immediate family members of Torstar Corporation, D.L. Blair, Inc., their affiliates, subsidiaries and all other agencies, entities and persons connected with the use, marketing or conduct of this Sweepstakes. All applicable laws and regulations apply. Sweepstakes offer void wherever prohibited by law. Any litigation within the province of Quebec respecting the conduct and awarding of a prize in this Sweepstakes must be submitted to the Régies des Loteries et Courses du Quebec. In order to win a prize, residents of Canada will be required to correctly answer a time-limited arithmetical skill-testing question. Values of all prizes are in U.S. currency.

Winners of major prizes will be obligated to sign and return an affidavit of eligibility and release of liability within 30 days of notification. In the event of non-compliance within this time period, prize may be awarded to an alternate winner. Any prize or prize notification returned as undeliverable will result in the awarding of that prize to an alternate winner. By acceptance of their prize, winners consent to use of their names, photographs or other likenesses for purposes of advertising, trade and promotion on behalf of Torstar Corporation without further compensation, unless prohibited by law.

This Sweepstakes is presented by Torstar Corporation, its subsidiaries and affiliates in conjunction with book, merchandise and/or product offerings. Prizes are as follows: Grand Prize—$1,000,000 (payable at $33,333.33 a year for 30 years). First through Sixth Prizes may be presented in different creative executions, each with the following appproximate values: First Prize—$35,000; Second Prize—$10,000; 2 Third Prizes—$5,000 each; 5 Fourth Prizes—$1,000 each; 10 Fifth Prizes—$250 each; 1,000 Sixth Prizes—$100 each. Prizewinners will have the opportunity of selecting any prize offered for that level. A travel-prize option, if offered and selected by winner, must be completed within 12 months of selection and is subject to hotel and flight accommodations availability. Torstar Corporation may present this Sweepstakes utilizing names other than Million Dollar Sweepstakes. For a current list of all prize options offered within prize levels and all names the Sweepstakes may utilize, send a self-addressed, stamped envelope (WA residents need not affix return postage) to: Million Dollar Sweepstakes Prize Options/Names, P.O. Box 4710, Blair, NE 68009.

For a list of prizewinners (available after July 31, 1994) send a separate, stamped, self-addressed envelope to: Million Dollar Sweepstakes Winners, P.O. Box 4728, Blair, NE 68009.   MSW7-92